Heather

Seven Sisters

Kirsten Osbourne

Sign up for instant notification of all of Kirsten's New Releases Text 'BOB' to 42828

And

For a complete list of Kirsten's works head to her website wwww.kirstenandmorganna.com

Prologue

Heather McClain looked at her sister Jessica as she got to the house where she'd grown up. "Do you have any idea why Dad called us here?" she asked. Her dad was always calling family meetings, usually so he could show off his newest tech gadget, but this time he hadn't said why they were all expected to be there. But as usual, he'd ordered, and his girls had obeyed.

"No idea. He's being closed-mouthed about this. Hopefully he doesn't just want to show us his newest game he's programmed for the Atari. I mean, I love video games as much as the next girl, but I don't need to see another golf simulator and be expected to get excited over it." Jessica was the second sister in the family of seven McClain daughters.

"I guess we're about to find out." Heather was the eldest, and she had a little house she loved right in the middle of Bagley, Texas. She had planned to spend the night curled up in front of the television watching *The Love Boat* and *Fantasy Island*. Saturday nights were the only nights when she took time away from her busy life to vegetate in front of the TV, and she hated that she'd been stopped. Thankfully she'd just gotten a VCR, and she could tape the shows and watch them later. Who knew how long her father would keep them there?

"How was aerobics this morning?" Jessica asked, looking at her sister out of the side of her eye.

"Ugh. I swear every woman in the world should not don a leotard simply because it's an aerobics class. Shorts and a T-shirt work just as well."

"You wear a leotard for aerobics class!"

"I'm the teacher! It's what I wear when I teach their darling daughters and granddaughters how to dance every day. Why shouldn't I wear one?"

"Why shouldn't they?" Jessica shot back with a grin.

Heather sighed. Sometimes talking to her sister was like talking to a brick wall. "I'm taping *The Love Boat* and *Fantasy Island* if you want to come over and watch them after whatever Dad has planned for us." She enjoyed watching the shows alone, but she knew her sister hadn't yet invested in a VCR.

"Ooh! Count me in! I can't believe Dad chose a Saturday night. Last time we told him he could never interrupt our Saturday night shows again."

"We'll live." Heather opened the front door and walked inside without knocking, knowing her mother expected it. "Mom! We're here!"

Her mother emerged from the kitchen, a grin on her face. "I was just microwaving some supper. I love how fast my new gadget works!"

"That's the next thing I'm buying myself," Heather said. "I want a microwave."

"The new ones aren't nearly as expensive as the radar ranges were in the seventies."

"I'm glad you're an eighties lady, Mom." Heather kissed her mother on the cheek. "Why exactly are we here?"

Her mother sighed. "You know your father. He has some new gadgets you all need to see as soon as possible."

"Oh, yay! Is Marti here?" Marti, the youngest sister, went to school in Austin, and she rarely made it home on weekends.

"She is. Your father said all seven of you needed to be here tonight." Mom led them into their father's study, where all of the sisters were waiting for the miraculous unveiling of *something*.

Heather went straight to her father, Robert McClain, and kissed his cheek. "Hey, Dad. What is so important?" She knew he wouldn't answer, but she also knew he loved to be able to hide his secrets. She was showing her love by letting him hide whatever he was doing.

"I can't say until everyone is here!" Dad said, his eyes still glued to his brand-new Macintosh.

Heather looked around her, quickly counting heads. She wanted to make it for her shows if at all possible. She had fifteen minutes. Maybe they'd all pile on the couch in the living room and watch. She touched her own chest, mouthing the names of her sisters as she went through them all. "Heather, Jessica, Gaylynn, Rebekah, Tracy, Candice, Marti." She shook her head. "We *are* all here, Dad. All seven of us, and we're dying to see whatever it is that you want to show us."

Dad grinned but shook his head. "We're doing this my way. You can watch your shows when they repeat." He looked around at all seven of his daughters, a look of pride on his face. "I have two new gadgets to show you, and there's another I'll be getting just as soon as it's available."

Heather and Jessica exchanged a look. They'd been right, but it was no surprise to either of them. "Okay, Dad, I'll bite. What are the new gadgets?" Heather glanced at her watch, saying a quick prayer that he would hurry, but she knew as well as her sisters did that it was not going to work.

"Not until I want to tell you. First, I'm going to tell you about what I don't have yet, but I will soon." He leaned back in his office chair, a huge grin on his face. He loved when all of his daughters were surrounding him. How could he not feel pride when they were all so beautiful and smart? "You know back in September, a plane was shot down in Soviet airspace, but it was an accident. You see, the Korean plane had never intended to fly into the USSR. They just went off course. Well, the US military has had a technology called Global Positioning Systems for years, and they've just opened it up for non-military use. Can you imagine what it would be like if we could just look at a gadget and know where we are? No man would ever have to stop and ask for directions again!"

"Like any man does!" Heather responded.

Robert glared at his eldest daughter. "I asked for directions when we got lost on the way to Yellowstone. Remember?"

"Dad, that was in 1972. More than ten years ago!"

He shrugged. "I keep a map in the car." He shook his head. "Stop trying to distract me, Heather! This gadget is going to change our world. I've already invested in a company who is working on the first handheld device. I can't wait!"

"Me neither," Jessica said, her face full of enthusiasm. Heather had always been impressed by Jessica's acting skills.

"So . . . the second gadget is even more exciting. With as much as you girls love telephones, I'm sure you're going to be super excited by this!" He held up an object that barely resembled a telephone. It was white, looked solidly made, and had an antenna sticking out of it. "I paid a pretty penny for this beauty, but it's a cell phone. I can make calls from my car with this thing!"

Heather looked at her sisters, surprised. "That's pretty cool!"

"I know! Let me show you how it works!" He punched buttons on the phone, and the house phone rang. Their mother answered.

"Hello?"

"I'm talking to you from a cellular phone."

"That's really nice, Bob."

"I want to try!" Marti said, reaching for the phone.

"No way!" Bob put the phone behind his back to hide it from his phone-hungry youngest child. "It's a buck for every two minutes you talk on it."

Marti immediately backed away. "I'm a college student. That's my food budget for a week!"

Everyone laughed, knowing she was exaggerating. "You should come to my place to eat after this," Heather offered.

Marti shook her head. "Nope. I'm staying here because Mom promised to do my laundry."

Heather looked at her mother. "You always spoil her. I was doing my own laundry at ten."

"And I can do my own laundry!" Marti protested. "But I came home for the weekend, and Mom said she would do it."

Heather rolled her eyes but didn't say anything else. What was the point? Marti would always be the spoiled sister. When Jessica looked at Heather, she could read her sister's mind. They'd always thought the youngest sisters had it too easy.

The next thing their dad did had them all gawking. He pushed a few buttons on his computer, and they could hear the sounds of dialing. "What are you doing, Dad?" Gaylynn, the third sister, asked. "That sounds like a phone call. How are you doing that?"

"I'm doing something that is going to change our world! I'm calling into a computer system that will allow me to talk to other people online! Soon, there will be no real mail! It will all be computer mail."

Heather shook her head. "I don't believe it. People will never give up writing letters to each other for typing things on a computer. It just won't happen."

"You mark my words, Heather. In another twenty years, people are going to be paying their bills online! I bet they will rarely talk to each other, because computers will be the favored way to communicate. Our world is changing, and that's all there is to it!"

Heather looked at Jessica, and she knew her sister was thinking the same thing she was. "Okay, Dad. Whatever."

As soon as the words left her mouth, there was a loud clap, sounding like thunder, and the lights went out. Their mother sighed. "It looks like all your gadgets blew a fuse, Bob. I'll go check the breaker." She picked up a flashlight they kept on the desk in his office, knowing he would need it. He was constantly making their power go out.

Heather stood there for a moment, feeling tingling throughout her body. "Does anyone else feel as if they got a little of the power that just went out? Like flung into their bodies?"

"Were you electrocuted, Heather? Are you all right?" Bob sounded very concerned.

"I think I'm fine. It wasn't so much an electrocution as it was a power surge." She wanted to say that it had the same feeling as when she'd gotten her first kiss, but she knew her dad would not approve. As far as he was concerned, she was thirty-two years old and had never been kissed. She wasn't going to disillusion him.

It was then that the lights came back on, and Heather saw that each of her sisters looked as shell-shocked as she felt. Maybe she would wait to watch her shows. "I'm not feeling great. I think I'll go home." It was then she noticed that her father had a reddish hue to his skin. It had never been there. When Mom walked back into the room, she had a blue hue. As soon as she walked close to their father, both of their hues blended beautifully, causing them to both look a bit violet. How odd.

Her mother hugged her. "Yes, go home."

Heather looked over at Jessica. "Come over tomorrow night. I'm not up for watching TV tonight."

Jessica nodded, looking a bit ill herself. "I'll be there around seven or so."

"Sounds good." Heather headed for the door, wondering what was going on. She was miserable all of a sudden. A hot bath and her bed were all she needed.

Chapter One

Heather finished her third class of the day and quickly mopped her face with a towel. The little ones were keeping her jumping.

Mrs. Jackson walked over, and Heather wished there was a place to hide. "I think that little Susie should be playing the part of the sugar plum fairy. She's the best dancer in the class, and you know it as well as I do."

Heather bit back a groan. "I've assigned the parts as I felt they needed to be assigned. I'm sorry if you're not pleased." The truth was, little Susie Jackson was the worst dancer in her four-year-old class. She danced into walls and fell on her butt more often than all the other girls in the class put together. And with a class of four- year-olds, that was truly saying something.

"There's a dance studio opening up in Nowhere. I'm sure the teacher there would recognize my daughter's talent for exactly what it is."

"I'm sure she would. If you feel led to take Susie there, I will understand. Maybe I'm just not the right teacher for her." Heather did her best to keep her face even. She knew that the true problem was that Susie had absolutely no natural talent and would be better off swinging a softball bat, but she couldn't say that to Mrs. Jackson.

Mrs. Jackson looked shocked. She was from one of the wealthiest families in Bagley. Of course, Heather was from *the* wealthiest family in Bagley. Her uncle ran a boys' ranch outside town, and they had always funded the place with their own money, though people in town rarely realized that. She'd be attending the annual fundraiser on Saturday afternoon. She'd cancelled all her classes and everything.

"If you don't want my business, then that's just what I'll do!"

Heather refused to back down. She'd known Angela Jackson since she was Angela Simpson and eating her boogers in kindergarten. "I'll miss you, Susie. Maybe we'll see each other around town though." She leaned down and hugged the little girl, who clung to her. "I hope you like your new teacher."

Susie's eyes filled with tears. "I like your class, Miss Heather."

"I like having you in my class, but if your mama wants you to go to the new school in Nowhere, I can't stop that from happening." Heather glanced at the clock on her wall. "I have exactly forty-five minutes to eat lunch before my next class is due." She turned and walked toward her kitchen, knowing it would infuriate Angela but not really caring. She'd never been the other woman's fan anyway.

"Come along, Susie!" The door of the dance studio opened and slammed shut.

Heather sighed. She walked into the kitchen and looked in the fridge. There was her grilled chicken salad she'd made for lunch. It had sounded great that morning, but now all she wanted was a taco. Tacos were her comfort food, and she was going to have one!

There was a small mom and pop place around the corner with the best tacos in Bagley. Maybe the best tacos in all of Texas. She shrugged her coat on over her leotard and hurried out the door. She didn't usually run around in just her leotard and tights, but she had no time to change if she wanted her tacos, and man did she want her tacos.

As she hurried, she watched people's hues. For the past seven months, every time she went out in public, she saw the hues of people. She could tell the people who were meant to be together by how their hues blended as they walked toward one another.

In front of her, for instance, were two perfectly good people, but when they were together, their hues turned black. It was all Heather could do not to tell them to stay far away from each other. She could see that the woman was pregnant, and she knew the fates would not be good to them. Black was always bad when it came to hues blending.

In front of the taco stand was a man with a hue like no other. The color hovering over him was a pure sky blue. She was drawn to it in a way she'd never been drawn to another. She didn't talk to him, though, because she had no time. As much as she wanted to get to know him, she knew he wasn't a local. She knew everyone who lived there in Bagley. Why would she want to start a relationship with a man who wasn't a local?

She stood behind him in line, and when he moved out of the way, she placed her order. Two tacos and a bean and meat burrito. And a Dr. Pepper. She knew she shouldn't have the sugar because she had to teach another three classes that afternoon and two that evening, but it couldn't matter to her. She needed that Dr. Pepper after her run-in with Angela. The woman had been a thorn in her side ever since kindergarten.

When she was handed her food, she turned around to see the man staring at her. He looked as flummoxed by her as she felt by him. "I'm Michael Muir," he said quietly, taking off his cowboy hat and tipping it to her.

"Heather McClain, but more importantly, I'm late!" Gripping her bag of Tex-Mex fabulousness in one hand and her Dr. Pepper in the other, she hurried toward the dance studio.

"What are you doing tonight?" Michael asked, obviously hurrying to keep up with her.

"Teaching dance. It's what I do every night."

"What about Saturday? Do you teach dance on Saturdays?" The man sounded slightly panicked as he tried to pin down a time he could see her again.

"Usually, but this Saturday, I'll be at the McClain Boys' Ranch. There's a huge fundraiser."

"May I escort you?" He stood outside the dance studio, obviously not wanting to go inside.

Her eyes met his, and she looked away for a moment, catching their reflections together in the plate glass window of her dance studio. His sky blue blended beautifully with her pink. The color was a shade of lavender that had always been a favorite of hers. It was even the color of the leg warmers she was wearing. "Meet me here at noon. You can drive me out there, and we'll spend the day together."

He grinned, tipping his hat. "I'll see you then, Heather McClain."

"And I'll see you, Michael Muir." She hurried inside and shut the door in his face. Five minutes to eat. She was going to be miserable all day, either from eating too fast, or not eating. She chose tacos over starvation and shoveled the food in quickly.

She had just finished the last bite of her burrito when the bell over the door tinkled, letting her know that the first of her afternoon students had arrived. She turned with a smile on her face and shrugged out of her coat. It was time for tap. She preferred ballet, but tap was fun as well.

Her mind was not on the children that afternoon, though. How could it be? Her brain was full of Michael Muir and only Michael Muir.

MICHAEL MET WITH JONATHAN McClain, following the man into the fields. "Are you any relation to Heather?" he asked, knowing it was probably a mistake. He was there to buy cattle from Jonathan, not to pick up women.

"She's my niece. Best dancer in the area. She was a Dallas Cowboys Cheerleader for a few years, but she didn't like how the women were treated as sex symbols. Said she was above that. Why?"

Michael smiled. He could just picture Heather in a Dallas Cowboys Cheerleader uniform, and he liked that picture. A lot. Maybe he could get ahold of one of the old posters she would have been on. "I met her in line for tacos a little while ago."

"Ahh. She must have taken a quick lunch. She usually eats in the studio."

"She said she was in a hurry." Michael tried to concentrate on the cattle he was there to buy, but he could only think of the beautiful niece of the man he was talking to.

Jonathan pointed out the bull he thought the other man would be interested in. "This guy is pure angus. He'd be perfect for the cross-breeding program you told me about."

Michael looked at the bull, which had been taken to a small corral on his own. There were two other bulls trapped similarly for his inspection. "Clean bills of health on all three of them?"

"Yup. These are the best I have. There are a couple of younger ones I'll use for my herd, but these are ready to go out and multiply other people's herds."

Michael looked around him. "You sure do have a whole lot of houses on your ranch." He wondered if this was the place Heather had told him about. The McClain Boys' Ranch. He knew he was dealing with a McClain, but how many McClains were there in the area?

"Yeah, those are the houses for the boys. I have seven sons, and those houses are for the foster sons on the ranch here. We keep about thirty at all times."

"That's really cool. I've never heard of a boys' ranch."

"We were certainly the first in the area. My grandfather started the boys' ranch part of the operation with his wife back in the early part of the twentieth century. Before World War I. There was a boys' orphanage in town, and when it burned down, my grandmother said she was taking all the boys in. So they set themselves up to raise them. Here we are seventy some years later, and the ranch is still raising boys at the same rate it raises cattle." Jonathan sounded blasé about the whole situation, but it was obvious he was proud of his heritage.

"That's interesting." And it made Michael certain he was buying his cattle from the right place. He wanted to help these people with their boys' ranch if it was at all possible. "Do the boys help with the cattle?"

"The boys help with everything. They have the same types of chores my own boys did as they were growing up. I have seven boys."

"Seven? That's a lot of boys."

"The seventh son in my family always has seven sons. Not a girl in sight. My brothers had lots of girls, but not me. Just boys. My brother Bob tried to one up me by having seven girls, but I had my seven boys, so it didn't work."

"I see." Michael found himself fascinated by the family. "I'm looking forward to getting to know you all better this weekend at the fundraiser."

"Are you coming?" Jonathan asked, seeming surprised.

"I'm going to escort Heather."

Jonathan raised an eyebrow before nodding. "Just know she has a lot of people who love her around here. Don't hurt her."

Chapter Two

Heather waited nervously in front of the dance studio on Saturday. She had taught her morning aerobics class, showered and changed, and was now ready. She'd insisted on a shower when she'd remodeled the old building to be a dance studio because she'd known she would want to shower between classes at times. Now she was thankful she'd done it.

When Michael walked up to her just before the time they'd set, his hue looked as pure as it had the first day. She'd been sure she'd imagined it. "Hi," she said softly. She wanted to hug him. Heck, she wanted to kiss him and see if what she was feeling was all in her mind.

"Hey there. Are you ready?" He looked her up and down, surprised at how good she looked in her jeans. She had looked pretty fabulous in her leotard and tights as well. She was wearing an old pair of jeans, a purple and pink plaid shirt, and a pair of cowboy boots.

She nodded. "This is a fundraiser my uncle does for the ranch every year. It keeps the boys in clothes and food." She couldn't tell him the full truth about the fundraiser, of course, because no one outside her family would really understand. There were strange things that happened within her family.

"Yeah, I bought a bull from your uncle Jonathan the day I met you, so I know a bit about the fundraiser."

"Oh, I didn't realize."

"Yeah, that's why I'm in town. I was looking for a purebred Angus bull to help my herd. I'm trying to go lower fat and cholesterol to make my herd more marketable."

"I see." Heather frowned. "Where do you live?"

"Idaho. A small little town called Muir. It was named after my ancestors there."

"Idaho?" She'd had no idea people really lived in Idaho. Well, in theory, she'd known of course, but she'd never met anyone from there. "It's cold there."

He laughed. "That's an understatement. We already have snow on the ground, and you're running around with no coat."

"I wore one the other day," she said. Of course, that had just been to cover up her leotard and tights. She didn't like running around town showing off so much of her body, which explained why she had only lasted a couple of years as a cheerleader for the professional football team.

"You did. I liked the leg sweaters."

She laughed, the sound tinkling through the air on their way to his truck. "Most people just call them leg warmers."

"Yeah, those things." He stopped in front of a big Dodge Ram with Idaho license plates. "Here we go. I hope you don't mind riding in a truck."

"Why would I? I'm a Texas girl. I just traded my truck in."

"You drove a truck?" He was surprised. Heather seemed so delicate to him, he couldn't imagine her driving a truck.

She laughed. "I drove a Chevy Silverado until a few months ago. Four-wheel drive and four on the floor."

He grinned. "Not many girls can drive a stick these days. I feel like it's a lost skill."

"My daddy made me learn to drive with a stick. He said there was no point in doing things halfway." She vaulted into the truck with no problem, and he was surprised by her ease. Sure, she was obviously athletic, but she was so petite he felt like he should tuck her in his pocket and carry her everywhere.

"Your daddy has a point." He got in beside her and started the truck, shifting into first gear. "Tell me about this thing we're doing."

"Oh, you'll love it. It's like an old town carnival. There's always a tilt-o-whirl and Ferris wheel. We can get hot dogs and cotton candy. It's just fun. The boys love to do it, and my aunt just loves to help organize the thing. They've been doing it since before I was born."

When they got to the ranch, he was surprised at the sheer number of people who knew her. "How do you know so many people?"

"Well, I've lived in Bagley most of my life. I left for a few years so I could try to do some professional dancing in Dallas, and I was a cheerleader there for a bit." She brushed her long blond hair out of her face. "But half the town is my family. It's ridiculous how many McClains are here, but the family tends to have lots of kids. I'm the oldest of seven girls."

"I come from a big family myself. Super tight-knit."

"Us too." She just wished he didn't live in Idaho. A rancher would never dream of relocating. She glanced at him again, surprised again at the pureness of his hue. She wanted to sink into him and watch their hues mix in a mirror, but her daddy would have a fit. She took his hand and led him over to where her mother was painting faces.

"Mom, this is Michael. He's visiting here from Idaho."

"Hello, Michael. Do you want me to paint a fairy on your cheek?" her mother asked, a twinkle in her eye.

"You know, I think I'm good! Thank you, Mrs. McClain."

Heather noticed her dad walking toward them, and for a moment, she looked for a place to hide, but then she realized that Michael could handle her father. If not, there was no point in even seeing him for the short time he was in Texas. "How long are you in Texas?" she asked, surprised she didn't already know. She wanted the answer to be forever, but she knew it wasn't.

He shrugged. "I was planning to leave yesterday, but I think I need to stay a little longer now."

"Who's taking care of your ranch?" she asked, surprised.

"My brothers are taking turns giving my hands their orders. They'll hold things together until I make it home."

Heather looked up as her father descended on them, his hand out to shake Michael's. "My brother told me you were in town. I'm Bob McClain."

Michael smiled. "I'm Michael Muir. It's good to meet you."

Bob looked into his eyes for a moment, studying the man in front of him. "I hear you're a rancher."

"I am. I have a modest ranch up in Idaho."

"Idaho? You're not thinking of trying to lure my baby out of Texas, are you?"

Heather laughed. "This is our first date, Dad. No luring is happening. Besides, I'm a Texas girl through and through. I couldn't imagine living anywhere else, let alone *Idaho*." The way she said the state name made it sound like it was a foreign country where people were known to torture their children and kick puppies.

"Idaho's not such a bad place," Michael protested. Already he couldn't imagine leaving Heather in Texas, but there was no way he could move there. He loved his home in a small valley in Idaho, where the mountains completely surrounded them. It might be over an hour to the nearest Walmart, but it was home.

"I'm not saying it is. I'm just saying it's not a place I've ever been . . . or ever thought about going really. Do people visit Idaho? By choice?"

He made a face at her. "I think it's a pretty wonderful place. I live in a beautiful valley there . . ."

"So does that make your sisters Valley Girls?"

"Not in the way you mean . . ." He shook his head. "Texans sure think their state is better than every other state, don't they?"

She giggled softly. "We don't think . . . we know!" Glancing over her shoulder, she saw her cousin Peter headed toward her with his fiancé, Lillian. They were about to get married and have seven more boys. Peter was the youngest, and everyone knew his fate. "Hey, Peter. This is Michael."

"Hi, Michael. I heard you just bought one of our bulls." Peter was in his mid-twenties, and there was a twinkle in his eye that made Michael wonder what the other man was up to.

"I did. I'm taking him back to Idaho with me even though Heather thinks Idaho is funny."

Peter grinned. "That's Heather for you. Her sense of humor has always been a little bit off. I have to say, I've never met anyone from Idaho. What's life like up there?"

Michael shrugged. He didn't feel intimidated by the man because he was holding the hand of a young woman. The man obviously didn't have feelings for Heather. "I like it. It's the most beautiful place on earth."

"You think? Have you seen a hill country sunrise yet?"

"I have. Just this morning. It was pretty, but not as pretty as the sun setting over one of the mountains in my valley."

Heather leaned toward Peter and Lillian. "His sisters are Valley Girls."

Lillian giggled. "I don't know if you should make fun of his home, Heather."

"I never did have a normal sense of humor. Peter said so, and he's known me since the day he was born. I wish I could say I've changed his diapers, because that would embarrass him, but I'm not that much older than he is."

Lillian shrugged. "You should probably say it anyway. Torturing your cousins should be your lifelong goal!"

"Cousin?" Michael asked.

Peter grinned. "Yeah, you bought the bull from my dad."

"Ahh. Are there any people here you're not related to, Heather?"

"Oh, maybe a few." Heather looked up as Jessica came toward her with their other sister, Gaylynn. "These are my sisters, Jessica and Gaylynn."

"It's nice to meet you," Michael said with a grin. He looked over at Heather, wondering if she was happy in the middle of her family reunion or if he should try to drag her away. "Are you hungry? I was thinking of getting a hot dog or whatever else I can find."

"Oh, I bet we can do better than that. There'll be some good Texas brisket around here somewhere."

"What if it's Idaho brisket?" he asked.

She laughed. "Like we'd import good beef. Texas is better than that."

He shook his head. "It's a good thing the rest of the country doesn't feel like you Texans do. I'd starve to death because I wouldn't be able to sell my cattle."

"You could just butcher them and eat them yourself, and then you wouldn't have to starve," she pointed out with a sassy grin.

"I could . . . I guess I'd be homeless then, which is worse in Idaho because the winters are brutal."

"That's all right. The summers in Texas are brutal." As they walked, Heather pointed out different people she knew. One little girl ran over and hugged her just as they were about to get to the barbecue stand. Heather hugged her back and smiled. "It's good to see you, Emily."

Emily didn't say anything else as she ran back to her mother. "One of your students?" Michael asked.

She nodded. "I love teaching dance. The kids are so much fun."

"I can see that. That one sure does like you."

"Emily likes everyone! She just loves to dance around all the time. I think she's the most natural dancer I have in all my classes."

"How old is she?"

"Six. She hates school, and she loves dancing." Heather stopped at the barbecue stand. "How about you let me choose for us? I promise, you need a Texas barbecue feast before you go back to your frozen northland."

"All right. That works for me."

Chapter Three

Michael enjoyed sitting at one of the picnic tables with her, eating the barbecue feast she'd insisted on. The brisket was to die for, but so were the baked beans and the potato salad. "Okay, Texas beef may not be better, but I have to admit that Texas *barbecue* is."

"Texas barbecue makes my heart sing," Heather said. She knew she should pretend that she ate very little, but she couldn't. She was an active woman who worked out hours and hours every day as she demonstrated dances for her students.

He grinned. "I think I can understand that." A moment later, they were joined by a group of young women.

"More of my sisters." Heather introduced her sisters in age order because it was the easiest way to make sure she didn't miss any. He'd already met Jessica and Gaylynn, and that left, "Rebekah, Tracy, Candice, and Marti. Marti's the baby."

Marti made a face. "I'm a baby who is going to school full-time. I'm not sure exactly how babyish that is. And by school, I mean the University of Texas."

Tracy wrinkled her nose. "I can't believe you're a Longhorn. You should have followed in my footsteps to become an Aggie."

"Whatever!" Heather rolled her eyes. "Growing up with six sisters is absolutely ridiculous. There's never any hot water. Your favorite sweater is always being worn by someone else."

Marti grinned. "I didn't do laundry until I went away to college because I just borrowed my sisters' clothes."

Candice sighed. "I *wish* she was kidding."

Michael looked at all of the sisters, wishing the other two were there. He was a bit overwhelmed, but he wanted to compare all seven of them. "It's nice to meet you all."

"Are you going to try to get Heather to go back to Idaho with you?" Marti asked. She had never been one to mince words, and she loved to embarrass her siblings.

"Do you think she'd consider it?" he asked.

"Probably not. She loves Texas. Besides, what football team does Idaho have for her to cheer for?"

"I haven't cheered in years," Heather said with a blush. "But I can't see myself leaving Texas." She looked at him, sitting there with his perfect sky-blue hue. She belonged with him, and she knew it. But how could she go so far from her family?

"I want to see a picture of you in your old uniform," Michael said, leaning toward her. "Do you still have it?"

"Yes, I still have it." She shook her head, blushing a little. "You know I quit the team because I didn't like being a sex symbol, right?" She wondered if he'd take the hint and change the subject. Hopefully he wasn't one of those men who was just trying to get into her pants. He didn't seem the type, but it was certainly possible.

"I do know, so I won't tease you about it." He took another bite of his barbecue, realizing that every one of her sisters were watching them. "What's there to do for fun in the evenings?"

"There's a dance club in town. It's not a bar, and they don't serve alcohol. It's truly just a place to go to dance." Heather grinned at him. "It's one of my favorite places."

"Do you want to go tonight?"

She frowned. "Tonight, there's a dance here. It's how we finish up the fundraiser. All of the single McClain boys and single McClain girls get to be auctioned off for dances."

"Hey, you have to dance with me. I brought you here!"

She tilted her head to one side, studying him intently. "Can you dance?"

He frowned. "Well, I can't do anything fancy, but I can hold a girl and dance with her. I'm not the guy you want to disco with . . ."

"Disco is dead." Heather leaned forward. "I'll give you a chance to dance with me, but you do have to bid on my dances. Think of the boys."

He sighed. "I guess I need to bid on your dances."

Heather reached over and covered his hand with hers. Would he try to kiss her as they danced? She was dying for that first kiss. She needed to know if the hues were right and he was meant to be her only true love. Though she had no idea how they could make that work. He was geographically undesirable. "Only if you want to dance with me." She knew she needed to start mentally preparing herself for when he went home to Idaho, but she wasn't ready. She wasn't sure she ever would be.

When it was time for the dancing to start, she stood on the stage with her sisters and their cousins. Each one of them would be auctioned off for ten dances, and the rest of the night would be their own. As she watched, Michael bid higher than anyone on her first dance. She went smoothly into his arms as if they'd planned it for years.

The song was "Almost Paradise," and she immediately rested her head on his shoulder as they swayed together to the music. He was so much taller than her five-foot nothing that she couldn't quite reach his shoulder and her head ended up on his chest. He made her feel so tiny and feminine.

At the end of the first dance, he leaned down and brushed his lips across hers. That kiss felt like more to her than any she had ever felt. The touch of his lips against hers set her whole body on fire. She let out a little gasp and wrapped her arms around his neck, kissing him back for all she was worth.

She only stopped when she felt a tap on her shoulder. She pulled away, afraid of who she would see. It was Peter. "Your dad is glaring at you something fierce. I'd back away if I were you."

Taking gulping breaths, she stared at Michael, wondering what on earth he'd done to her. He had made her feel as if she was in someone else's body.

Peter grabbed her hand and pulled her to the stage, jumping down himself. Now that he was engaged, he didn't have to have a dance auctioned off like the other cousins did.

Heather stood staring out at the group of people unseeingly, taking gulping breaths of air. How on earth was she going to be able to dance with someone else now? She'd never be able to let him go. Never.

On the drive home, she was silent. It was hard to know what to say when she knew she was falling deeply in love with a man who lived over a thousand miles away. At least she thought it was over a thousand. Idaho seemed like a far-off planet.

When he got into town, he asked, "Where do you live? Should I take you home?"

It was hard to answer. She wanted to wallow in self-pity, though she wasn't a wallower. How could she be in love with a virtual stranger who wasn't even a Texan? "Yes, please. I'm just around the corner. I walk to my dance studio most of the time."

He followed her directions, pulling up in front of her small house. The house she had so lovingly decorated. The house that now felt so empty because he didn't live there. What was wrong with her?

"Do you want to come in for a drink?" She didn't know where the words had come from and immediately wanted to take them back. It was their first date. She shouldn't be taking him inside.

He got out of the truck and silently followed her inside. Once he'd shut the door behind him, he turned to her and asked the question that had been on her mind since their kiss. "What are we going to do?"

Heather shook her head. "I have no idea. I run a business here."

"And I have a ranch in Idaho. I can't really spend time away, and neither can you." He put his hands on her waist and drew her to him, his lips taking hers in a swift, deep kiss. "But . . . we can't ignore that!"

"No, I knew when I saw you in line at the Taco Hut that we were meant to be together." She buried her face against his chest, not wanting to think about saying goodbye. "How much longer will you be here?"

"I have no idea. None. I really was supposed to take my bull and leave yesterday. My brothers are wondering what my problem is, but I told them I met a girl . . ."

She laughed. "And they knew then you'd never come home?"

"Nah, I'll go home. I have to." He turned from her, running his fingers through his hair. "It's Saturday night. I'm supposed to be home watching *Love Boat* and *Fantasy Island,* but here I am with some girl I barely know, and all I want to do is stick her in my pocket and take her home to Idaho with me."

"Your pockets aren't big enough for me. I have muscles!" She flexed one bicep and made him laugh. She did have muscles, but they were very different than the kind of muscles he had. His were from hours of hauling hay and herding the cattle. Hers were from dancing.

"Nice muscles. I bet you could help haul hay!"

"Or you could dance with me!"

He kissed her again. "We're both going to need to do some serious thinking about what we want from each other. I don't know if we can make forever a reality."

"But that's what I want." Her voice was barely a whisper, but he heard her.

"Me too. I don't think it's an option." He left quietly, closing the door behind him. She was fascinating and wonderful. How had she known they were meant for each other before they even met, though? That didn't make sense.

He slowly headed to the only hotel in town, parking his truck out front. When he walked in, he went past the front desk, and after a moment of contemplation, he stopped. "Do you know the McClains?"

The girl at the desk grinned at him. "Everyone in town knows the McClains. Everyone in this part of the state knows the McClains. They're wonderful people."

He frowned. "Do any of them ever move away from here?"

"You must be the man who was dancing with Heather all night. Rumor has it you two couldn't keep your eyes off each other."

He frowned. "How did you know that?"

"It's a small town. People make note of everything and talk about it. It's part of our way of life."

He groaned. "Lovely. Yes, I do mean Heather. What are the chances I can get her to move to Idaho with me?"

The girl's eyes widened for a moment before she shook her head. "I don't think there's any chance at all. She's happy here. She loves her family, and she runs a business. I think you need to move here."

"I own a ranch in Idaho."

"You can't sell it and buy a ranch here? That's what it would take for the two of you to be together, I think."

He sighed. "I have a feeling I'm going to spend the rest of my life alone." He walked away, noting the girl's nametag read, "Beth." Why couldn't he fall for the Beths of the world? No, he needed Heathers. He needed the girls who were impossible.

Chapter Four

Heather fell asleep that night with her thoughts on Michael and only Michael. He was the first thing she thought of when she woke up. She wanted to find out all she could about his town in Idaho, but she couldn't imagine leaving Bagley. Her family had been there for generations, and leaving the people she loved was absolutely out of the question.

She dressed quickly for church, knowing her family would worry if she didn't go, but what she really wanted to do was stay home and eat ice cream and tacos. Lots of ice cream and tacos. Her family was known for always finding their perfect match, but she wasn't sure that was going to include her. Her perfect match lived much too far away. Deep inside her she knew that there was not another man on the planet who would be as good for her as Michael was.

She ate a quick breakfast of instant oatmeal and decided to walk to church. Sunday was the only day she didn't really work out, so she always wanted to walk a few extra steps to get some sort of exercise in. She believed that her body was a temple, and she treated it as such. Well, where exercise was concerned. Food was all about sacrificing to the temple.

She stepped onto her front porch and immediately spotted Michael sitting in his truck out front. He was dressed in a suit and tie and saw her as she saw him. He stepped out of his truck. "Do you want a ride to church?"

Heather shook her head. "I like to walk to church. It's my only real exercise on Sundays." Well, that and housework, but who wanted to admit to that?

"I'll walk with you then." He walked toward her and took her hand in his. "Do you mind if I go to church with you?"

She sighed. "In a town this size, going to church and sitting beside a girl is tantamount to announcing your engagement."

"I'm good with that."

"I'm not. I don't want people thinking I'm dropping everything and moving to Idaho, and I don't want people to think you're coming here." She took a deep breath. "I'm not sure it's a good idea for us to spend so much time together when we both know it's all going to end in heartache anyway. You're not moving here, and I'm sure not moving there."

Michael frowned. He couldn't imagine that he could find the girl of his dreams and just walk away, not even getting to know her. "Maybe we're both wrong, and we'll get on each other's nerves within a week. Don't you think we owe it to ourselves to make the breakup earlier if we can?"

She laughed. "You know as well as I do that's not going to happen."

"I do. But it was worth a try." He didn't know how to convince her to move to Idaho, but he knew he couldn't move to Texas. "You know, there's no dance studio in the town I'm in. I'm sure there are closer dance teachers here . . ."

"Do you have any idea how hard it's been for me to get my business off the ground? Do you think I need to be the one to move because I'm the woman?"

Michael bit his tongue. He wanted to tell her he thought she should move because he had ancestral land, but he was sure she didn't want to hear that. "Not at all. I just think it would be easier for you to find another building to run a business from than it would be for me to move thousands of head of cattle."

Heather knew he had a point, but she didn't have to like it. "We'll see." She stopped in front of the church and walked toward the building. She had no idea what religion he was, but at the moment, she didn't care a whole lot. As they walked in, she headed straight for her family. All of her sisters were in town for the weekend for the fundraiser, and it was always fun for them to sit together.

She saw Peter and Lillian talking to Marti. "Now that the fundraiser is over, I can put all my energy into planning the wedding," Lillian said softly. "And into convincing Peter that it really is a good idea for me to name our seven sons after the boys from *Seven Brides for Seven Brothers*. I don't know why he's not just jumping at the idea."

"He has no taste," Heather said, jumping into the conversation. *Seven Brides* had always been one of her favorite movies. "Some of the dance moves in that movie are epic!"

Lillian linked her hand through Heather's arm. "See? Heather knows what she's talking about! And if I have to have seven sons, I might as well name them something fun."

Peter groaned. "I feel ganged up on."

"That's what I'm here for!" Heather said with a grin.

Marti laughed. "Of course we're going to side with Lillian. We're welcoming her to the family. Making her one of us."

"What if I want to name one of my sons something else?"

"Why would you?" Lillian asked. "Adam, Benjamin, Caleb, Daniel, Ephraim, Frankincense, and Gideon are the best names ever!"

Heather heard Michael give a choked laugh, and she turned to wink at him. "Maybe if you'd be willing to compromise Frankincense to Frank, Peter would agree . . ."

Peter sighed. "Yes. I refuse to name my son Frankincense."

Michael clapped his hand on Peter's back. "I have a feeling you're stuck with the other names. Of course, she's willing to have your seven children, so I think you just nod and agree."

"If I agree, I'm afraid she may make me sign a contract agreeing to name them those ridiculous names."

Lillian pulled a sheaf of papers from her purse. "I had them adjust Frankincense to Frank when they wrote up the contract. You just need to sign here." She pulled a pen out as well and handed it to him.

Peter looked at Heather. "Can you believe this? She doesn't want a prenuptial agreement. She just wants me to sign off on what our kids will be named!"

Heather shrugged. "She sounds smart to me." She wandered off to where her parents were standing together, hugging her mother. She wasn't sure if Michael was still acting as her shadow, but she could only assume he was.

"It's good to see you again, Mrs. McClain, Mr. McClain."

Bob looked at Michael. "Are you making an announcement by attending church with my daughter?"

"I'm announcing my intentions for certain. She doesn't seem to agree at the moment, but I'm hoping she will."

Heather didn't dare look at Michael, feeling too much frustration she was certain would show. Already her feelings for him were so strong . . . and yet she wasn't willing to pick up and move her entire life to Idaho for him. "Have you heard what the sermon is about today?" she asked her mother softly.

Her mother's eyes moved from Michael and back to Heather before answering. "I think it's on loving your neighbor."

"I always like those sermons." Heather sat down in the pew behind her parents, knowing it was reserved for her and her sisters.

Michael sat beside her, frowning at her. "Are you angry with me?"

Heather lifted her hand to run her fingers through her hair but thought better of it. Her hairspray wouldn't hold if she did that, and who wanted flat hair? "I'm confused with you. I don't know what you want from me. I've told you I'm not willing to move to Idaho, and yet you're still here, talking to me and trying to convince me to do it."

"I'm not trying to convince you to move to Idaho. I'm trying to convince you to give me a chance and let me spend some time with you while I'm here, so we can see if either of us will need to consider moving across the country or if we should be happy where we are."

She turned to look him in the eye. "I just don't think I'd ever be willing, so I feel like the two of us spending a lot of time together is just going to lead to heartache."

"I'm willing to give it a shot if you are." Michael held his breath while he waited for her answer. His family had always been very intuitive, and he knew she was the only woman who he needed by his side for the rest of his life. He'd known it from the moment he'd set eyes on her.

She sighed. "I guess we can spend a little time together today and see where it goes."

He took her hand in his and squeezed it. "Thank you. Right now, that's all I'm asking for."

Thankfully, the pastor stepped up to the pulpit then and announced the first song they'd sing. As she stood beside Michael, she wondered who was watching them and their little declaration. After a moment, she decided it didn't matter and instead concentrated on singing. If someone had something to say, they could just do it. Her reputation was impeccable.

By the time church was over, she was feeling comfortable with her decision to spend some time with Michael. There were plenty of things to do around town, and she liked the idea of being with him.

As soon as the sermon was over, he turned to her. "What are your plans for the day?"

"I usually spend Sundays at home doing laundry and housework."

"I'll help then."

She frowned. "I figured you'd come up with something more interesting than that to do!"

He shrugged. "All I care about is spending time with you. What we do with that time doesn't matter at all to me."

Heather sighed. "Well, we need to get lunch first. I can feed you for supper, but I have no idea about lunch. I usually just go to my mother's for Sunday lunch after church."

Her mother turned to them. "Michael, you should come to Sunday lunch. You might feel a bit overwhelmed by the sheer amount of estrogen in the room, but I would love for you to be there to get to know us all better."

Heather looked at Michael, waiting for his response. On one hand, she would have liked a private meal with him, but on the other hand, she knew that the less time they spent alone together, the better it would be for her heart.

"Sure, I'd love to have lunch with you."

Heather nodded. "We both walked, so we'll head over." Bagley was small enough that walking from one end of town to the other took less than twenty minutes.

"All right. I'll have Marti set an extra plate."

"Don't tell me . . . she traded you setting the table today for her laundry?"

Her mother grinned. "How'd you guess? You can't begrudge me taking care of my baby!"

"No, I guess I can't." Heather shrugged at Michael. "My youngest sister is rotten."

"Sounds like it." Michael couldn't help but laugh at the expression on Heather's face. She looked disgusted with the trade her mother had made with her sister.

The two of them talked to people on their way out of the church. Heather found herself introducing Michael over and over. A couple of the other young women seemed to be eyeing him, but Heather didn't care. She knew he would be loyal, though how she knew it, she didn't know. None of their hues were right with his either. No, he was meant for her. That much was obvious.

As they walked away from the church, she kicked at a rock. "I think church went well. Mom is excited to have you come over for lunch."

"Your family seems really nice. Even your spoiled sister."

"Don't you think she's rotten?" Heather asked, grinning at him.

He laughed. "Maybe. A little. I don't really know her." He was afraid to say anything bad about her sister. If her family was anything like his, he knew that it was okay for siblings to insult someone but not for outsiders. He would do anything to avoid making her angry. Other than stay away from her, of course. That wasn't an option.

Chapter Five

When they arrived at Heather's parents' house, the others were already there, and the house was bustling with activity. Jessica was in the kitchen helping cook, and Marti was setting the table. Tracy was sitting with the newspaper, reading through everything there was. Tracy sold cars for a small car dealership in town, and she did a great job of it. She always said her dream job was to own an Irish pub in town, but Heather couldn't really see that happening.

As soon as they walked in, Gaylynn hurried over. "Come and sit in the living room with me. Dad has the Cowboys game on, and I want to get to know your guy."

Heather frowned. "I wouldn't exactly call him mine."

"I would. I'm hers. No one else's. I'm going to convince her to marry me if it takes all week." Michael was grinning as he said it, but he was dead serious.

Gaylynn laughed. "All week? You're giving it a whole lot of time there." Gaylynn was a mental health counselor, and sometimes she made Heather nervous. She hadn't told anyone in the family about the colors she saw hovering over people's faces, but she knew her sister would think she was insane if she did.

Michael shrugged. "I'm an optimist. What can I say?"

"An optimist? I'm a realist," Heather said softly.

Gaylynn laughed. "You? A realist? You're more of a pie-in-the-sky optimist who believes in any dream there is out there. Why would you even think you're a realist?"

"Oh, hush. I'm not that bad."

"You definitely are! You were told you couldn't ever dance after you broke your leg when you were little, and you worked every day until you could dance. You were told you could never make the Dallas Cowboys Cheerleaders, and what did you do? You went out there, and you made it happen."

"And that makes me a pie-in-the-sky optimist? I would think that would make me an achiever."

Gaylynn shrugged. "That too. You should come see me this week. Something's bothering you."

Heather rolled her eyes. "I don't need help from you to figure out what's bothering me. I know that well."

Michael looked between the sisters. "What does that mean?"

Gaylynn smiled sweetly. "I'm a mental health counselor. I have an office in town, and Heather thinks she doesn't need someone like me in her life."

"That's not true at all. I need my sister. I know that with everything inside me." Heather stepped close to Gaylynn and hugged her tightly.

Gaylynn smiled. "Fine. You need me as a sister but not as a counselor. I get it. If you change your mind and want to talk, you know where to find me."

"Always." Heather knew her sister had her best interests at heart. It must be obvious how she was feeling about her new relationship with Michael.

Their dad was sitting there in the living room, a pad of paper in his hands. "I'm sure there's a way for me to figure out who will win the Superbowl early in the season if I can just make the right algorithm," he mumbled.

"If you ever get that algo figured out, I'd love to hear about it!" Michael said, sitting down and pulling Heather down beside him on the couch. He wanted to put his arm around her, but he really wasn't sure how her father would feel about that.

"I will. If I figure it out. *When* I figure it out."

Heather watched the television, thrilled that the cheerleaders were on. Several of her closest friends were still on the squad, and she watched them whenever she had the chance. It made her feel connected to them. As she watched, one of her friends was in the front for a fun routine that Heather had written herself. She was sad not to be there to perform with them, but she was so happy they continued it without her.

Michael looked between the television and her family, watching all the sisters. They all seemed like they were in their own worlds to him. "What do you do for a living, Mr. McClain?"

"Call me Bob. I'm a video game designer. Atari." He had a silly grin on his face as he named the biggest video game company there was.

"Oh, really?" Michael knew about Atari, of course, because everyone did, but he wasn't really a fan of video games. "Have you ever thought about creating a realistic hunting game?" Hunting was one of Michael's favorite activities. He was always thrilled to take his mother enough meat to last an entire winter. He was careful to use every bit of the animal, though, just as the Native Americans had. He thought it was best not to waste anything.

"I've messed around with it a little. I figure if someone is that into hunting, they won't be sitting around playing video games. Instead they'll be outside enjoying themselves. Am I wrong?"

Michael grinned. "Probably not."

"Well, then why should I make it? That makes no sense, now does it?"

"I guess not. It would be something that could get me to at least try a video game. Shooting aliens is really not my thing."

Bob frowned. "I didn't work on any of the alien games. I'm more the golf guy and the bowling guy."

Michael shrugged. "Those are probably more fun than the alien games."

Heather was thrilled when her mother stuck her head into the room to call them for lunch. She wasn't sure her dad and Michael were going to come to an agreement on anything, and she knew any arguments at the table would be stopped by her mother.

AFTER THE MEAL, HEATHER helped wash the dishes while Marti introduced Michael to the glories of the Atari golf game. He played to appease Heather's father, but he was not a fan. Not at all.

As they walked back to her house, he said, "What's on our agenda for the rest of the day?"

She frowned. She could do most of her housework late at night but not the laundry. She needed clean leotards to teach in that week. "I need to get some laundry done. I have *Love Boat* and *Fantasy Island* taped from last night. We could watch it while I work on laundry. I'll have to pause it some . . ."

"That's fine. Wow. Laundry day is exciting." He needed to do laundry as well, but he'd do his at the hotel the next day while she worked. He wasn't wasting a single moment of the time they had together. He had to convince her that the two of them together were more powerful than any job.

She made a face at him. "Just don't think you're going to get to fondle my panties . . . or my leg warmers. Got it?"

"Yeah, sure, whatever." He grinned at her, glad she was still willing to tease with him, despite her misgivings about their future.

When they got to her house, she settled him on the couch while she wandered into her bedroom to gather her laundry and get it started in the garage, where her washer and dryer were.

When she walked back in, she pushed play on the VCR, and then sank onto the couch beside him. "This is last night's shows. I hated missing it, but I am so glad I have a VCR." She glanced over at the kitchen to see her microwave oven on the counter. She loved being an eighties woman. So many gadgets to make her life easier.

He scooted a little bit toward her and slipped his arm around her. She looked at him for a moment. "Thanks for not doing the yawn and stretch. It seems like your style."

"Smooth and sophisticated?"

She laughed at that. "Sure. That's what I was thinking." She snuggled closer to him, her head going to rest on his shoulder as she focused on the show. She loved how many people fell in love every single week.

She got up twice to deal with laundry in the middle of the shows, but when they were finally over, she looked at him. "I've been working on a jigsaw puzzle, if you like them."

He grinned. "One of my favorite things."

She stood and led the way to her kitchen table. "My table is always covered with a jigsaw, so I always end up using my lap as a table."

"Doesn't bother me," he said, liking the way she did things. He wasn't exactly formal either.

Together, they sat and worked on the puzzle, talking about random things. "How old were you for your first kiss?" he asked.

She tilted her head to one side, pretending to have to think about it. "I was fifteen, and it was after my first football game where I cheered on the varsity squad. It was Brian Angles, and he kissed me under the bleachers. I was sure my mom was going to see us when she picked me up, but she didn't." She looked at him. "What about you?"

"I was sixteen, and it was after homecoming. I kissed her on her parents' front step, and her dad came out and told me to get off his porch." Michael frowned. "She was grounded for two weeks, and then we went out again, and I kissed her again. I learned to do it before pulling onto her father's land, though."

She laughed softly. "Wise move. What was her name?"

"Tina Nelson. We dated for the rest of the schoolyear, and then she moved away."

"Do you still think of her?"

He shrugged. "Only when someone is asking about my first kiss. She didn't exactly rock my world. She was nice, though. And she was great about helping me with my trig homework. I was not good in trig."

"You dated a girl for her math abilities?"

"Well, yeah. Why did you date Brian?"

"Because he was the only sophomore with a car, of course!"

They both laughed. Priorities were so different when you were in high school than when you were an adult. "Are you going to spend time with me tomorrow night?"

She frowned. "I have evening classes tomorrow. I have morning classes as well but no afternoon classes. We could have lunch."

"You have a difficult schedule," he said with a frown. Thankfully he wasn't working while he was in Texas, and he could accommodate her.

"Yup. I try to make it easy for all the moms who want their daughters in dance. Some want their kids to nap all afternoon. Some are coming right after school. I have different hours on different days." She rubbed the back of her neck. "I would hate to leave my students." She knew he didn't understand, but she wished he would. Those kids and parents counted on her.

"I know you would. Are there no other dance schools?"

"There's one in Nowhere, which isn't terribly far, and I know the teacher. She'd be good with the kids. It would just feel weird to abandon students I've been teaching for so long."

"How long has your studio been open?" he asked.

"Only three years, but many of my students have been with me since day one. I truly love what I do."

"I know you do." He thought about whether or not he had ever seen a dance studio in Muir or any of the neighboring towns. "I really think you could start a place near me. You could be happy there."

"I have to be here at least until early December. I have promised to do The Nutcracker with my students." She wouldn't commit to anything after that, but she couldn't even consider leaving before.

"Maybe you could come visit me over Christmas. My mom would love to have you stay with her, so there are no strings. Just a visit."

She frowned. "I've never been away from my family for Christmas. I guess I can think about it, but I have a feeling I'll want to be here."

He nodded. "I can understand that. I do want to show you Idaho, so you can see that it's not as horrible as it is in your head."

"Maybe after the play. I could come in mid-December."

He really hoped they'd be engaged by then, but he was willing to wait for her. Whatever it took. "Whenever is good for you. The cattle and I are willing to host you anytime, day or night."

She grinned at that. "Well, I do want to see the valley you keep talking about. And the Valley Girls."

"I wonder how my sisters would react if you called them that."

"No idea, but I have this weird feeling we're going to find out."

He laughed. "Probably." He covered her hand with his, looking into her eyes. "I really don't want our relationship to be over before it starts. I think we can work it out."

"I hope so," she said softly. It was then she realized that he already held her heart in the palm of his hand. If only he had been there three years before. Before she'd started her dance studio. When she'd been at a crossroads trying to decide what to do. Before.

He leaned over and brushed his lips across hers. "I think you're pretty special, Heather McClain."

She studied him for a moment, mesmerized by the pretty blue hue covering his face. "Do you believe in the supernatural?"

"You mean like *Twilight Zone* stuff?"

"Sort of . . ." She hadn't talked to anyone about her seeing the colors on people, but for some reason she wanted . . . no, she *needed* to tell him. "About six months ago, I started seeing strange hues on people. Like their faces were weird colors."

"Okay . . ."

"And I realized that if two people get close to each other, their hues will blend. Sometimes they change to a lilac color, which means they belong together, or a black color, which means they do *not* belong together . . . or something in between, meaning they're neutral together." She rushed through her explanation, looking only at her hands, and then she looked up at him, wondering if he'd think she was insane.

"That's odd. It never happened before that?"

She shook her head. "There was a power outage at my parents' house when Dad was showing us some weird gadgets. It's been happening ever since."

He frowned. "What do your parents say about it?"

"I haven't told anyone but you."

He shrugged. "It doesn't bother me if that's what you're trying to find out. All the twins in my family have magic powers."

"You have lots of twins?"

He nodded. "We tend to. And all of them have weirdness going on. I'm not a twin, so I don't have it, but my mother is. She told me before I left Idaho that this trip would make me either the happiest man alive or the saddest. She said to fight for what I needed."

"Really?" She was surprised but not terribly. The youngest of the seven sons always had powers in her family. Why not his, too? She wondered if other families had those secrets they never told.

"Really. What color is our hue together?" Michael asked. He knew she'd have the answer, and he suspected he knew what it was. No wonder this was so hard for her.

"Lilac. Your hue is a beautiful shade of blue. I noticed your hue before I noticed you, and I was so drawn to it."

"So that means we need to marry, right?"

She sighed. "It means we are *very* compatible. I don't know if there can be more than one person with a hue that matches another."

"You haven't seen that?"

She shook her head. "I don't know that I believe there's one soulmate for everyone either. I mean, what would happen if you were married to someone else when you met your soulmate? How heart-wrenching that would be!"

"Now I want to go for a long walk with you and ask you about the hues of everyone we see. Can you see it on television? And in pictures?"

She shrugged. "I couldn't until a few days ago. Now, I can. I don't know why or how it changed, but it's weird."

"Do you have any idea how badly I want to take you to the airport?" he asked.

Heather frowned at him. "Why do you want to take me to the airport? That makes no sense."

"Because of all the people who are reuniting after time apart. I love watching people at gates of airports. They run into others arms, and there's so much kissing. It's weird, but it's like *the* place to watch for people."

She grinned. "That could be fun. Figure out who really belongs together and who shouldn't be together. We could go around offering free relationship advice, telling people they should break up with their significant other or they should be with them forever."

He laughed. "I can picture doing that. I wonder if going to the movies would have the same effect. Is there a theater in town?"

Heather grinned as she understood. "We can sit in the back row and check the others out." She went to pick up her paper. "Let me see what's playing!"

Chapter Six

That evening was filled with hilarity as Michael and Heather sat in the back row of the theater, and Heather pointed out couples who would last and those who were most likely to kill one another. Neither of them were able to focus on the movie, *Irreconcilable Differences,* because they were too busy laughing.

"It's a good thing no one around us is watching the movie," she whispered. "They'd all be angry with all our giggling."

"Real men don't giggle. They chortle."

Once the movie was over, he walked her home.

"That was fun," she said. "It never occurred to me to do something like that. I've been too busy adjusting to seeing weird stuff."

"I can understand that." He stopped at her door, wanting her to invite him in but knowing she needed to work the following morning. "I'll pick you up for lunch. What time?"

She frowned for a moment, thinking about it. "How about noon? We can get tacos and go to the park for our very own picnic."

"I'd like that." He leaned down and brushed her lips with his. "I'll see you tomorrow. Wear some exciting leg warmers for me."

"You know I will!"

Heather watched him go, thinking about how much she wished they had more time together. He was a good man, and she wasn't ready for him to go back to Idaho. She wanted to yell at the unfairness of finding the man of her dreams and him living so far away.

The following day found Heather walking on air—or dancing on air, as the case may be. Her students giggled as she forgot the steps a couple of times, but none of them said a word.

When it was finally time for lunch, she locked up the studio and hurried out to get into Michael's truck with him. "Tacos!"

He laughed. "I think you only like me for the food I provide . . ."

"Like you provide food often. I provided food yesterday—well, my parents did, and that's pretty much the same thing."

"Hey, I'm providing food today. Tacos."

"What if I want a burrito? Or chips and queso? Or a combination of all three?"

"Get whatever you want. You know I'm not going to complain." He paused for a moment, looking at her before pulling out of the spot in front of her studio. "Well, I won't if you kiss me."

She laughed and scooted across the bench seat, lifting her lips to his. "I was confused as I danced this morning. All the kids were giggling as I tried to teach them the wrong steps."

"Oh? And why is that?"

"Because I couldn't stop thinking about you. Why are you in Texas for such a short time?"

"Because my life is in Idaho." He wanted to say more about how her life could be there, too, but he sensed it wasn't really time yet.

They picked up the tacos and headed for the big park at the center of town. It was filled with walking trails, and there were plenty of picnic tables. It would be a little chilly, but Heather didn't care. Spending time with her man in the middle of the day was worth anything.

She grabbed the bag with the food while he took the drinks, and they carried them to a picnic table at the edge of the woods. She sat down and divvied up the food, taking the burrito and chips and queso she'd decided on. Michael handed her the Dr. Pepper and frowned. "How can you drink that swill? I don't even like kissing you after you've had it in your mouth."

She raised an eyebrow. "Are you going to let that stop you?"

He laughed. "You know me better than that."

"I do know you better than that! How are things going at your ranch?"

Michael frowned. "It's been a couple of days since I checked in with my brother. I should call after I drop you off."

Heather nodded. "You probably should. I can't imagine trying to be away from my studio for that long . . . well, if there was a break in classes I could. I like to have a couple of long breaks every year to rejuvenate myself."

"Then you can spend those breaks in Idaho. It's been decided."

She laughed. "You really think I'm just going to obey that way? You don't know me at all yet, do you?"

"I guess not!" He watched as she finished her burrito, and then the two of them cleaned off the table, throwing their trash in a nearby can. "Let's go for a walk."

"Sure." She didn't say that she got enough exercise by teaching because she truly believed that everyone needed more than what they got. Always. "This is my favorite park. We used to come here in high school and walk. Well, my friends and I did. The kids who were into parties had better places to go."

"I can see that. In Idaho the kids went to some of the mountain parks and had parties there. They always left a big mess, and the locals always complained about them, claiming they were city kids who had no respect for nature."

"So would I be considered a city kid?"

He shook his head. "Nah, your town is too small for that. You'd have to be from a big city like Dallas to qualify as a city kid. Why? Would you have partied in the mountains?"

Heather shook her head emphatically. "No, and I wouldn't leave my trash if I did. I don't believe in littering and leaving messes for others. I've been taught this little thing called responsibility. I think it's important."

"Sounds like we have the same ideas on child-rearing. Wanna have babies?"

She felt a tear pop into her eye, realizing that what she wanted more than anything would be to have babies with him. If only he was local. "Yeah. I do want to have babies."

"Does that mean you'll marry me?"

She shook her head. "Honestly, if you lived closer, I'd run away to Oklahoma and marry you this afternoon. But you live in Idaho. Who lives in Idaho?"

"Are we back to that? Idaho is the most beautiful place on God's green earth. Come visit and you'll see what I mean."

She sighed. "I think maybe I will come up after we perform *The Nutcracker* in December. I'll have a full month off before we start getting ready for the spring shows, and I need to see where you live."

He grinned, taking the hand he was holding and bringing it to his lips. "I'd love that." In his mind, he was already thinking of a place for a dance studio for her. Surely, she'd agree to move to Idaho if he had a place where she could work and do what she wanted to do happily.

She had no idea what was running through his mind, but the goofy grin on his face told her that she wouldn't like it. "That's not an agreement to move to Idaho and have your babies, you know."

"I know. But it's one step closer, and I believe in taking things one step at a time. We'll get there. I promise you."

Heather wished she felt as strongly about it as he did. She wanted to spend forever with him, but she just wasn't sure they could make it work. Idaho to Texas was such a distance. She'd never see her family again. "I honestly don't know if moving across country is something I can ever agree to. I love my family too much."

"I know. We'll make the decisions together." He didn't want to think about what it would mean to her to move, just as he didn't want to think about what it would mean to him. If only one of them had a job that was easier to transfer.

After dropping her back at the studio, he headed to the hotel to catch up on his laundry. He'd only brought a few changes of clothes, and everything that wasn't on his back was dirty. As he walked into the hotel, Beth was at the front desk. "Mr. Muir! You have a phone message."

Michael walked to the front desk and took the message. It said to call home. It was an emergency. He frowned. No one in his family would insist he call home unless it was something real. None of them were given to drama.

"Thanks, Beth." He took the note and hurried to his room, pulling his calling card from his wallet as he rushed through the hall. He dialed his mother's number, knowing she'd know whatever it was that was going on. "Hey, Mom. It's Michael. What's wrong?"

"Joshua got kicked by that stallion he's been trying to tame. Three broken ribs and a concussion. He can't cover for you anymore, and honestly, he needs you to help cover for him."

Michael frowned. His brother had been trying to tame a stallion for months, and it hadn't been going well. He didn't know why the idiot didn't just give up. "All right. I'll sleep for a bit and leave tonight."

He could hear his mother's sigh of relief. "Thanks, Michael. We'll make it up to you."

"I know." He hung up the phone and rubbed his hands over his face, glancing at the clock. Heather's class didn't start for another twenty minutes. He could hurry to her, tell her what was happening, and then sleep until he had to leave. Oh, and he needed to arrange for the bull to be in the trailer he'd brought with him. He sighed. It was time to get back to the real world and stop living in his little world of romance.

WHEN HEATHER GOT HOME from work that night, her house felt so empty. The previous day had been all about her and Michael, and now here she was, alone. She had his address to write to, but he wouldn't even be home for a couple of days. How she wished her dad's computer was hooked up to more computers nationwide, and then they could at least message each other without long-distance bills.

Instead of thinking about how much she already missed him, she hurried around the house, doing the chores she'd put off on Sunday so she could spend the day with him. Chores were boring, but at least she wasn't dwelling on her Michael.

IT WAS THURSDAY EVENING when Heather's phone rang. She had been jumping at every little sound, hoping he would call her. "Hello?"

"Hey there. I made it home safe and sound. I just needed to hear your voice before I sleep for a few hours and then get back to work."

"It's good to hear your voice, too," she said softly. "I miss you." She probably shouldn't admit it, because surely for both of them it had just been a quick vacation fling. Well, a vacation fling for him and a quick romance for her. It couldn't last. Could it?

"Come see me in December. Please. I'll even buy your plane ticket. You just give me the dates, and I'll make it happen."

"I'll buy my own plane ticket, thank you very much!"

He chuckled softly. "Does that mean you'll come?"

She sighed. "Yes, I'll come. What airport should I fly into?"

By the time they'd hung up the phone, she had given him the exact days she planned to be there. She would call a travel agent the next day. She couldn't give up on him, no matter how far away he lived.

After the call, she sank down onto her couch and looked at a calendar. Six weeks. It would be six weeks before she could see him and touch him and hug him. It would seem like a lifetime.

HEATHER THREW HERSELF into her work. Every waking moment was spent at the studio or planning her lessons. And she started thinking about people she knew who could take over the dance studio if she left. She made a few calls to different friends she had cheered with, and she found one who was definitely interested.

"I do need to see if I feel the same after I see him next month," she explained to Tricia when they met for lunch. "It might be completely different."

"Do you really think that's even possible?" Tricia asked. "It sounds to me like you knew it was love from the first moment you set eyes on each other."

"Well, yeah, but that doesn't mean that it won't be different. Maybe absence is making the heart grow fonder. When I see him, maybe I'll realize he's not a friend to those with noses, and he drools."

Tricia laughed. "If that happens, I'm going to be shocked. You never even noticed when the head quarterback noticed you. You're not falling for some Idaho rancher without a real reason."

Heather headed back to the studio after her lunch with her friend, knowing she was right. She needed to admit it to herself. She was in love with a man who lived very far away.

As they got closer to the performance, her nerves started to get the better of her. She wanted to be with Michael. They talked every Friday night for a little while, but neither of them wanted to waste the kind of money it would take to talk more than that.

The Friday before the pageant, he called at eight, as he always did. "Hey you!"

"Hi! How're the cows?"

"They're good. How're the kids?"

"Getting on my last nerve! They are forgetting all their dance steps, and the performance is next week!"

"I know it is. And you're going to be here two days later. I have a calendar, and I'm crossing off the days."

"Is your mom still okay with me staying with her?"

"Of course she is. She's so excited to meet you, it's ridiculous. I might be a little excited myself."

She laughed. "Maybe I'm a little excited. I do miss you. Terribly. You can't possibly be as wonderful as I remember, though, so I'm sure that it's going to be different once I get there."

"It better not be. I expect you to walk off that plane and run into my arms, kissing me madly! If you wanted to just tell me that you were moving to Idaho then, it would be acceptable."

She shook her head. "You're a mess, Michael Muir. Do you know that?"

"Yup. I do know that. But I'm *your* mess. What else could you ask for?"

"I'll see you soon. Ten more days."

"That's ten days too long, but I'll have to deal with it." Michael's voice was sad but excited all at once. He felt the same as she did. That they were meant to be together.

Chapter Seven

When Heather got off the plane in the Salt Lake City airport, she was exhausted, but her eyes scanned the crowd, looking for the familiar face she so badly needed to see. Her parents weren't thrilled about her flying across the country, but they knew at her age, they had little they could say about it.

As soon as she saw Michael standing off to one side, his cowboy hat in his hands, she rushed toward him, dropping her carryon bag at her feet as she flew into his arms. After they'd embraced for a moment, he whispered, "We need to hang out watching other couples. See if we should let them be together."

She laughed softly, lifting her face for his kiss. "You know what? I like the way you think."

"That's a good thing. I would hate it if you thought I was insane."

"Well, let's not go that far . . ."

He leaned down and picked up her bag, nodding in the direction they needed to walk. "Let's get out of here. It's a three-hour drive to Mom's house, and it's already four in the afternoon. We don't want to get hit by a snowstorm."

"Is it snowing?" She hadn't even thought to look. She had been more focused on him than she'd realized. She glanced toward the window, but she couldn't really see much. The tarmac was clear, but the mountains in the distance looked snow covered. Of course, for all she knew, they were snow covered year-round.

"Not at the moment. There's a dusting on the ground, though, and a little more at home. Do you drive in snow?" he asked.

She shook her head. "I never have. When it snows in Texas, the entire world shuts down. When would I learn?"

"Well, the world doesn't shut down for snow around here," he said with a grin. "Let's go get your stuff." They'd agreed she'd stay for a week, getting to know his family and the area.

She was excited to finally be with him but nervous as well. What if his family didn't like her? "Your mom really doesn't mind me staying?"

"Are you kidding? She's been after me to marry for years. She heard there was a woman coming to visit me, and she was walking on air. She even made a new quilt for the spare room for you."

"I hate that she went to that kind of trouble . . ."

"Trust me. She was thrilled to do it."

They got to the baggage claim, and she spotted her suitcase pretty quickly. She walked over to pick it up, but his hand was there before hers. "I got it. You just step back."

She grinned. As independent as she was, she'd always wanted to be with someone who would take care of her. It was odd, and she knew it. "Thank you."

As soon as they were in his truck, she leaned back, looking all around. "I didn't realize that Salt Lake City was surrounded by mountains. It seems like there should be a huge lake and nothing else here."

He laughed. "I can see that, but there are mountains in every direction."

"It all looks amazing." The mountains weren't the kind she'd seen in Colorado; they were more of a black rock and not nearly as pretty in her opinion.

"Are you hungry? Did you eat on the plane?"

"I had some pretzels. I'm due for a real meal."

"Okay, we'll find something."

"Is your mom expecting us to eat there?" she asked.

"Nope. I told her you'd probably be hungry when you got off the plane."

Heather grinned over at him. "You think you know me so well."

"I do know you well." He reached over and entwined his fingers with hers. "I'm glad you're here."

"I am, too. I feel out of my league, and it's weird that I'm staying with your mother, but I'm glad I'm here." She rubbed the back of her neck. "Tell me about your family."

"My dad died about five years ago, and I now run the family ranch. I'm the oldest son. I have two brothers and two sisters. My sisters are super excited to meet you. Karen is married with two little ones, and Isabelle is in college, but she's out for the semester."

"I'm sorry about your father."

He nodded. "He had stomach cancer. By the time they caught it, it was way too late." Michael had always felt like his father had been taken from him way too soon, but he didn't add that. He wasn't ready to talk about that with anyone outside his family. He pulled off the interstate and onto a side street, heading for a small family-owned restaurant. "I love to come to this little café whenever I'm in Salt Lake. Do you trust me?"

"I sure hope so since I just flew across the country to see you."

He grinned. "I guess you do." Pulling into the parking lot of the place, he stopped the truck. "Have I told you yet how happy I am that you're here?"

"Once or twice. Tell me again!"

"I'm happy you're here!"

She grinned, getting out of the truck and walking around to the front to meet him, their hands gripping one another. "What kind of food do they have here?"

"It's a little Italian place, and the family who runs it is actually Italian. They have the best chicken fettuccini alfredo I've ever had. And the garlic bread is to die for!"

"Sounds yummy. I'll give it a try."

Once they were seated with their menus, she read hers over, deciding that she would go with his suggestion. She put the menu down and saw him watching her. "I can't believe we're actually together again," she said softly. "It felt like it was never going to happen."

"How was the recital? Did the kids do well?"

She nodded. "They did really well. I was getting nervous toward the end there because none of them could seem to remember the right places to put their feet . . . but when it all came out in the end, it was great. The children were sweet, and their parents were thrilled." For a minute she considered telling him about Tricia being ready to take over her school, but she changed her mind. She wasn't quite ready to tell him, because she needed to know if he was serious about her first.

For a little while as they sat waiting for their food, there was an awkward silence, but then they both started talking at once, and it was as if they'd never been apart. "How's your brother feeling?" Heather asked.

"Oh, he's fine. Trying to train that stallion again. I really wish he'd sell the thing and be done with it. I don't know why he's so obsessed." Michael shook his head. "He was sorry to pull me away from you so quickly, and he's excited to get to know you."

"I'm looking forward to meeting everyone."

"Good because Mom has a party planned for tomorrow evening. She's having everyone over for a game night. If you can survive a Muir game night, then you're in."

"In what?" she asked.

"No idea, but you're in it!" He grinned at her, taking her hand in his. "The drive to my house is long, and we're an hour behind you. You may want to sleep while I drive."

She shook her head. "Nah. I'm too nervous to be tired."

"Nervous? About what?"

"Meeting your mother. Do you have any idea how many men have taken me home to meet their mothers?"

He frowned. He didn't like thinking of her with any other men. He was feeling very territorial where she was concerned, and that was a new thing for him. "How many?"

"None. You're the first, so meeting your mother makes me nervous. Doesn't that make sense?"

"I guess it does." He grinned at her, pleased with her answer. "I've only met the mom of one of my girlfriends. Well, one since high school."

"And who was that?"

"You. Don't you remember?"

She laughed. "I thought you meant other than me. Stop trying to mess with my head!"

During the long drive, she regaled him with the errors her students had made during the ballet. "And then little Susie tripped over her own feet and fell into Abigail, who fell into Tiffany. It was pretty funny."

"No one was hurt I hope?" he asked, grinning at the picture her words painted.

"Nah. I wouldn't be laughing about it if one of the girls had been hurt. It was just silly."

"Did you bring your leotard?" he asked.

"Nope. I left it in Texas, but I did bring my leg warmers. I figured I'd need them here more than there."

He turned the car into a long driveway with a huge house at the end. "I live in the guest house at the back of the property. Mom is still in the main house. This is my ranch." He looked at it through a stranger's eyes, noting that it was time to replace the sign out front.

"It's huge." Her own parents' home was half the size.

"Come on. Mom's waiting up for us." He grabbed her luggage from behind the seat and led her to the front door, knocking once and going in. "Mom! We're here!"

An older woman with short brown hair and green eyes hurried into the kitchen. "You must be Heather!"

Heather nodded. "Yes, ma'am. I appreciate you letting me stay with you."

"You are welcome any time. I've seen how happy knowing you has made my Michael."

"He's made me happy, too." Heather glanced over at Michael, who was looking everywhere but at her.

"I'm going to take your luggage to your room. You two get acquainted."

Mrs. Muir walked over to the stove. "I'm going to make some tea. Would you like some?"

"I'd love some. It's a little colder here than I'm used to."

"Yes, I heard you're from Texas. It's a lot warmer down there. It's supposed to get down to five degrees tonight."

Heather shook her head. "I can honestly say that I don't ever remember being anywhere that cold."

Mrs. Muir poured tea into cups and served it with some cookies. "I hope you're not always watching your figure, because I do like to bake."

"I probably would be if I didn't dance as hard as I do. When you're always twirling around, you don't tend to put a lot of weight on." Heather did weigh a little more than she had when she was cheering but not much. She was happy with her weight, which she knew a lot of women couldn't say.

"Good. I wouldn't want to see you skimping on my yummy baked goods."

Michael arrived back in the kitchen then and sat down with them. "Thanks for the snack, Mom."

"No problem. I'll eat with you two and then show Heather her room. You two have been alone for long enough today, and now you get to share her."

Heather grinned, loving that Michael's mother wasn't afraid to give him her opinions of anything. "I am pretty sleepy."

"I'm sure you are. What time did you have to wake up to catch your flight?"

"Six. I had a layover in Dallas Fort Worth, but it was a straight shot from there. It's been a very long day."

Michael frowned at her. "I wasn't thinking about how long you'd been up. You should have told me to grab fast food so you could get to bed sooner."

"Why would I do that? The Italian place you took me to was amazing. I'm fine. I'm not working in the morning, so I have all the time in the world."

He grinned at that. "Are you happy to be off work for a while?"

She nodded. "I do love my students, but every once in a while, I need to be able to sleep late."

"I can understand that." He covered her hand with his. "Plan on sleeping late tomorrow. I'll be up before dawn as usual for work, but you don't have to do anything while you're here."

Heather frowned. "I'm sure I'll at least help your mother with cooking and take some of the burden of having a houseguest off of her."

"You will not!" Mrs. Muir exclaimed. "I'm thrilled to have you, and you will be lazy this week. It's your job."

Heather grinned. "Being lazy has never been something I'm good at."

"I have a good library of romance novels. You are welcome to immerse yourself in them."

"I could do that." Heather actually liked the idea of having some time to read. She couldn't help but wonder how much time she'd have with Michael while she was there.

"I want to show you around town at lunchtime tomorrow. There's a little café that's good, and we can explore." He didn't add that he had a surprise for her, because he wasn't sure if she was ready.

"That sounds like fun." Heather hid a yawn behind her hand. "I'm sorry. I'm sleepier than I realized."

His mother got to her feet. "Come with me. I'll show you your room. You'll have a private bath and a nice big guest room."

"Sounds nice." Heather smiled at Michael. "I guess I'll see you tomorrow."

He nodded. "I'll come by for you around noon."

"I'll be ready." She wanted to lean down and kiss him goodnight, but she didn't want to do it in front of his mother. It would just be too awkward.

He seemed to agree. He squeezed her hand as she walked by. "Goodnight."

"G'night." Seeing him again made all of the old feelings rush back. She hoped she could sleep instead of lying in bed all night staring at the ceiling and thinking of him. He would certainly be on her mind a lot, though she wished it was different.

Mrs. Muir led her to a large bedroom on the second floor of the house. There was a bathroom off the bedroom. "There's another bedroom that connects to this bathroom, but no one is staying there. This big old house is lonely now that all my kids have flown the coop."

"You have a beautiful home." Heather couldn't imagine living alone in a place like this, but she had to admire the older woman for keeping it so clean.

"It'll be Michael's as soon as he marries. I'll move into the guest house, and he can rattle around in here."

Heather frowned. "I think you should get to keep your house."

"But there's only one of me, and when he marries, I expect there will be more than two quickly." Mrs. Muir gave Heather a probing look that had her blushing. Yes, she wanted to be that wife. Yes, she wanted to have those children.

"It will be a change for certain."

"Yes, it will." Mrs. Muir stepped toward the doorway. "I'm just down the hall if you need anything."

"I won't be afraid to ask." Heather watched as the door closed and then went for her suitcase. Jammies and bed were all she could think about at the moment.

Chapter Eight

When Heather woke the next morning, she looked around the room, her eyes still wanting to stay closed. There was a moment of panic as she tried to remember where she was, and then she fell back on her pillows. Idaho. She was in Idaho, and she'd be spending her day with Michael. Well, part of her day, anyway.

She glanced at the clock on the nightstand and saw that it was just past nine, and she climbed from the bed. That was after ten her time, and she couldn't remember the last time she'd slept so late. After a quick shower, she dressed and made her hair full and pretty.

She walked down the stairs, not knowing what she'd find. Mrs. Muir had seemed so nice, but Michael had been present for most of their interactions. Heather hoped the older woman would be just as nice when he wasn't there.

When she reached the kitchen, a cheerful Mrs. Muir grinned at her. "I hope you slept well!"

"I did. Thank you." Heather desperately wanted to make a good impression on Michael's mother, but she wasn't sure how. How do you make the woman who is your potential future mother-in-law happy?

"Sit down! I have a couple of muffins for you and a cup of coffee. Are you a coffee drinker?"

Heather nodded. "Not always, but I do enjoy a cup from time to time. I'm not one of those people who has to have it within thirty-six seconds of falling out of bed or her day is ruined, though."

Mrs. Muir grinned. "I can usually last forty-three seconds before I ruin my day over coffee." She placed two blueberry muffins on the table in front of Heather along with a cup of coffee.

"Thank you. I didn't mean to sleep so late."

"Nonsense. You were tired, and you had every right to sleep as long as you needed to." Mrs. Muir got herself a muffin and a cup of coffee and sat down across from Heather. "Michael should be here in an hour and a half. He's excited to show you our little town."

Heather took a sip of the coffee, liking how it filled her with warmth. She would have been just as happy with hot tea or hot chocolate, but the coffee was good, too. "I'm looking forward to it. He thinks a lot of this place. He talked about it all the time while he was in Texas."

"I'm sorry we had to call him home early. We honestly needed him here."

"I understand completely, though I would have liked a little more time with him." Heather shrugged. "Family first, though."

"I appreciate you understanding. We'd have expected you to do the same if it had been one of your sisters. Michael says you're the oldest of seven girls."

Heather nodded. "I am. The youngest is in college."

"Do you think you'd be able to move away?"

"I really don't know. I love what I do, and my business is doing well. It seems like it would be crazy to leave it at this time." But it might be crazier not to.

"Maybe it would. Maybe it wouldn't. I know that I would think it was crazy to have love in the palm of your hands and let it go. I'd have given anything for just a few more years with my love."

Heather frowned. "Michael told me his dad died young."

"He did. And I made him wait a couple of years to marry so I could finish my college degree. I never used that degree because I immediately became a housewife and then a mom. I should have married him as soon as he asked." Mrs. Muir stared off into the distance as she spoke. "I'm not telling you what to do, Heather. I just don't want you to have the kind of regrets I have."

"Thank you." Heather didn't know what else to say. The warning was understandable, but she hoped nothing like that ever happened to Michael. She knew it would tear her up.

"Everyone will be here tonight. You'll get to meet all four of my other children. I thought I'd make a nice supper and then we'll play some games. I have Trivial Pursuit."

Heather grinned. "I love that game!"

"I do, too. It's so fun. I always feel a little slow, but we play in teams, and that helps." Mrs. Muir leaned forward, as if to impart a secret. "I sometimes read through the first thirty or so cards in each box so I'll have a fighting chance."

Heather giggled, covering her mouth with her hand. "I'll never tell!"

"Good girl. I knew I liked you." Mrs. Muir got up then and started to clean up the small mess they'd made. "Michael should be here in an hour. You might want to wander around outside for a bit . . . explore."

Heather nodded. "I'd like that a lot." She hurried upstairs and put on her outside gear. When she was covered with leg warmers, a coat, gloves, a hat, and scarf, she went back down the stairs and stepped outside. It was snowing lightly, and Heather wanted to spin around, trying to catch snowflakes on her tongue.

She'd seen snow a few times, but it was sticking to the ground here and looked like they may even get enough for a snowman. She had always wanted to build a snowman!

She wandered around to the back of the house and found a small path that led back through some trees. There she found another house that was much smaller. She looked at it for a moment, contemplating. *It must be where Michael lives,* she decided.

There were no festive decorations on the smaller house as there were on the bigger one. Someone had gone all out to decorate the big house for Christmas, and she knew that someone was Michael's mother. This house looked like a bachelor lived in it. There wasn't even a wreath on the door, and she highly doubted there would be a tree in the house.

It made her sad to think that he didn't even decorate for Christmas. At home, her house was completely decked out for the season, inside and out. She knew she wouldn't actually spend the holiday at home, but she'd instead go to her parents' house as she did every year. That didn't matter about the decorations, though. She was happy to put them up.

Suddenly she wanted to decorate with Michael. She wanted them to have a home together to decorate every year. Glancing over at the big house his mother lived in, she knew it would be theirs. Well, he did have to ask her to marry him first, but that was just a formality as far as she was concerned.

Heather continued on her walk, daydreaming about someday having his baby. Even though she wouldn't be surrounded by her family, she would still be surrounded by *a* family. Michael's family would become hers. There was no doubt in her mind.

She was just walking back around the front of the house when she spotted his truck parked out front. "Michael!" She raised a hand and waved to him.

He grinned at her. She was definitely dressed like a Texas girl in an Idaho winter. She was covered from head to toe by thick, warm winter clothing. He'd never seen anything like it. Well, he had but not at a balmy twenty-eight degrees. "You ready?"

She nodded. "I don't have my purse. Do I need it?"

He shook his head. "I can't imagine why you would. Unless you want to try to drive in the snow."

"No, thanks. I have no desire to drive in the snow."

"All right. Climb in then." He slid behind the steering wheel and headed toward town. "I thought we'd drive through town, and I'll show you everything, and then we'll have some lunch."

"Sounds good. Your mom fed me muffins when I got up, which was after ten. I felt like a sloth sleeping that long. I can only imagine what she thinks of me."

"You're not a sloth. You were up early yesterday, and you've been going non-stop getting ready for the recital." Michael shook his head. "You had the right to sleep late."

"Yeah, but not every day. I want to be able to work with you at least one day while I'm here."

He frowned at her. "You want to do ranch work with me? Really?"

"Why not? I helped on my uncle's ranch growing up. It's not like I don't know what I'm doing around a cow or horse."

"Well, if you really want to, you're welcome to join me one day. If you get too tired you can always go back to the house for a nap."

Heather looked at him for a moment in disbelief. "Is that a challenge?"

Michael looked at her, just then realizing how his words must have sounded. "Not at all. I'm sorry if that sounded condescending."

Heather folded her arms and looked out of the window on her side of the truck. She wasn't sure she was pleased with him at the moment.

When he reached town, he pointed out all of the important things. "That's the grocery store. We have a butcher in town as well. There's a small car dealership if you like Jeeps." He pointed out the post office and a couple of small restaurants as they drove. "We even have a dime store."

She took in everything, liking the look of the old brick buildings in town. "How big is this place?"

"About twenty-five hundred people. Not big, but not too terribly small either." Michael hoped she liked it, because he needed her to stay there with him and not spend the rest of her life in Texas. He pulled into a small café that had the best food in town, and he got out of the truck. "I figured we'd eat here. There's a pizza place, too, and you can always eat at the bowling alley, but this is my favorite."

Heather got out and walked to the building with him. When they walked in, he was greeted by name. "Hey, Michael. Just pick a table. I'll be there in a minute."

Michael nodded and led Heather to a table in the corner. "I went to school with her older sister," he said about the waitress.

"Is there anyone in town you don't know?" she asked.

"Maybe a few people. I do know most." The waitress came over then, looking at Heather with unashamed interest. "This is Heather. I met her while I was in Texas in October."

"Someone said you were twitterpated. It's nice to meet you, Heather. I'm Brandi."

Heather nodded. "It's nice to meet you, too."

"Is this your first time in Idaho?"

"Yes. It's a beautiful state."

"I agree, but then it's home." Brandi gave them each a menu. "What do you want to drink?"

"Dr. Pepper?"

Brandi shook her head. "We have Coke, Sprite, root beer . . ."

"Coke is fine." Heather wasn't sure if she could live in a town that didn't have Dr. Pepper at every restaurant. They'd better not eat out much.

After Brandi walked off, Heather studied the menu. "What's good?"

"Pretty much everything." Michael closed his menu and pushed it away. He always got the same thing, and he wasn't sure why he even bothered to look, but every single time he reread the whole menu, looking for hidden gems.

She finally closed her menu, realizing the little restaurant was jumping. The waitress was rushing around. "It seems like a nice town."

"Trust me, it is. I can't imagine living anywhere else. I mean, your town was nice and all, but with no winter, I don't think I could live there."

She glanced out the window and saw that the snow was still falling. "How deep does it get before people stay home?" she asked. In Texas, a state of emergency would have been called with the amount of snow on the ground already, and it didn't look like it was stopping anytime soon.

"A foot or more probably. I never really thought about it. My truck has four-wheel drive, and I just go when I need to."

When Brandi came back, she ordered a club sandwich and the soup of the day, which was baked potato soup. After the waitress had hurried off, she leaned forward. "Am I allowed to make a joke about eating potato soup in Idaho?"

"I wouldn't recommend it!" He grinned. "Actually, we embrace our potato-loving ways. Potatoes are a staple crop around here. People from all over come to help with the potato harvest."

"Interesting," Heather said with a grin. "I guess if you grow good potatoes, you might as well brag about it."

"Trust me. We do!" He took her hand in his. "I have a surprise for you after lunch. Do you like surprises?"

She frowned at him. "I'm not sure. It depends on the surprise."

"Well, I hope you like this one then. I worked hard on it."

"Then I'm sure I'll be pleased with it." She had no idea what it could be, but she wasn't going to complain. He'd thought about doing something special for her, and that was all that really mattered. "I want to see a picture of your parents together later, if you can find one. After listening to your mom talk about your dad today, I want to check out their auras."

"Sounds good to me. I also want you to tell me if you think my sister's new boyfriend is worth anything. She met him at college, and we're all meeting him for the first time tonight. Tell me if he's good for her, and I'll know whether or not I should scare him off."

She laughed softly. "I guess I could do that. What about your brothers? Are either of them bringing dates?"

He shook his head. "Nah. No one would ever go out with those two losers."

Heather smiled. "Sounds like a brother talking there."

"Well, I am a brother. A good brother, too."

"I'll keep that in mind. What's the surprise?" Heather had learned that if she distracted her father when he was talking about a surprise, but then turned the conversation back to it, he was more likely to spill the beans.

"I'm not telling you that! That's why it's called a surprise. You'll just have to see for yourself." Michael frowned at her. "Are you trying to use your voodoo on me? Because it won't work."

"The only voodoo I have is knowing if people belong together. I couldn't use voodoo on you if I wanted to."

"Good. I wouldn't want that."

Heather put her hand in Michael's and smiled. "No voodoo for you."

Chapter Nine

After lunch, they got back into the truck, and Michael drove Heather to a part of town they hadn't yet been to. There was a huge building on the main street through town that he stopped in front of—a for rent sign on the dirty window. "There's a real estate agent meeting us here in a few minutes."

"A real estate agent?" She gaped at the building, realizing then what he'd meant it for. He wanted her to rent it as a studio.

"Don't you think it would be perfect for teaching young dancers?" he asked. He wanted her to be at home there, and for her being at home meant that she would need to have an occupation.

"You're being awfully presumptuous, aren't you?" Forget that she'd made the decision that she would stay in Idaho as his wife if that's what he wanted just hours before. The fact that he would just assume she would move across the country for him made her angry.

A car pulled up behind them, and a middle-aged woman got out, walking up to the truck. "Hi, Michael. Is this Heather?"

Heather couldn't help but wonder what the woman had been told about her, and she wanted to be angry, but she didn't think the woman deserved to treated badly simply because Michael had overstepped. "Yes, I'm Heather McClain."

"It's nice to meet you. Michael has said wonderful things about you. I'm Janet Jensen. Do you want to see it?"

Heather nodded, smiling politely, but inside, she was seething. He hadn't even asked her to marry him, and there he was trying to get her to start a business in Idaho. Now that she thought about it, she wasn't sure they'd ever talked about marriage. They'd talked about making lives together, but did he realize that meant marriage for her?

She got out of the truck, not allowing herself to look at Michael. Stepping into the building, she could see it had been vacant for some time. "What was it used for?" she asked.

"It was a saloon at one point. It'll need some major renovating to make it into a dance studio, but I think it could happen. Michael and his brothers could supply the labor. He's already been all over the building, trying to make sure it would work. There's even a little apartment above the store that you could rent out or use as a place for your down time. Maybe a lunch room and a place to have meetings. An office."

Heather traipsed through the old building, following Janet everywhere. She made all the right noises and smiled at the right times. She was aware that Michael was behind her the entire time, but she didn't dare turn around. She was too annoyed with him at the moment.

As she walked through, she couldn't help but picture it after it had been converted to a dance studio. She could see a barre where the bar was. She stifled a laugh when she realized she would replace a bar with a barre. Oh, her sense of humor was ridiculous at times.

When they had finished touring the building, Janet stopped in front of the bar, and she spread out some information on it. "The building can be purchased or rented." Two figures were named, and both seemed to be terribly inexpensive to Heather.

"I'm going to have to think about it. I didn't realize I was going to look at a building today, and I don't have a loan in order or anything . . ."

"The money would be taken care of if you were interested in this property," Michael said softly.

"As I said, I'll need to think about it." Heather's voice was curt, and she hoped he realized she was annoyed with him. She certainly wanted him to realize it.

Janet smiled at her and nodded, obviously understanding they needed to talk. "Michael has my number. You just let me know if you need anything at all, and I'll be around."

"All right."

"Is it okay if we stay a while longer so she can see what I was thinking for it?" he asked softly.

"Of course." Janet put the key in his hand. "Make sure I get that back by the end of the day. You can put it in my drop box at my office." With those words, she left the building, leaving Heather and Michael alone.

"Why are you upset with me?" Michael asked softly.

Heather folded her arms over her chest. "I'm a little annoyed that you just assumed that I'm moving here. When did you set this meeting up?"

"Last week, but—"

"But? You decided that you had the right to decide not only that I will give up my life in Texas and move here, but that you got to pick the building where I'd work? Are you *kidding* me?"

He frowned. "I was just trying to help you see that you could make your dream work as well in Idaho as you can in Texas. Does it really bother you that much?"

"I just think you should have asked me if I wanted to see buildings while I'm here. I don't know why you thought it was okay to take it upon yourself to make such major decisions for me."

"I'm not making decisions for you. I'm showing you that you have options here as well as you had at home. That's all. If you hate it that much, we can leave, and I won't show you what I was thinking for the space."

She sighed, still annoyed, but not willing to bite off her own leg from annoyance. "Fine. Show me what you were thinking."

Michael wasn't sure why she was upset, but he decided it wasn't the right time to propose to her. He had the ring in his pocket, and he'd planned to drop to one knee as soon as Janet left.

Instead, he took her arm and guided her through the building she'd just seen but talked about what he saw in each room that would benefit her. "I think this is as big as the studio you had in Texas, right?" he asked as they finished the tour.

Through his eyes, she could see it all, and it was amazing. She wanted to stay, and she wanted to teach dance there. "Are there even enough children who would want to learn to keep me busy?"

"I've been asking around town. One of my sister's friends teaches at the local elementary school, and they even sent home a form to be filled out to determine interest. There are thirty-four school-aged girls who are interested in taking dance. I know of at least twelve pre-school girls. And that doesn't count junior high and high school. I think you would be kept as busy as you wanted to be. I even mentioned to a few women that you taught an aerobics class in Texas, and many of them want that as well."

"You've put a lot of thought and a lot of work into this, haven't you?" All at once, she felt horrible for getting so angry with him for assuming she'd move there.

"I have. I wanted you to know exactly what you'd be looking at if you decided to move here. You do have options."

Heather walked into his arms and rested her head on his shoulder. "I'm sorry I got angry with you."

His arms closed around her. "I think we're both feeling a bit overwhelmed. We only have six more days together. The week is going to go by too fast, and then you'll be back in Texas, and I'll be here, missing you all over again."

"Just in case, I found someone who could take over my school in Texas," she said softly. "We cheered together, and I know she would be wonderful with my students."

He looked down at her, his face lighting up with excitement. "You did?" He was thrilled to hear she was thinking the same way he was, making plans for any eventuality.

"I did. I told her it wasn't a for-certain thing because I didn't know if we'd still feel the same when we saw each other again, but she's standing by and ready if we decide that I should come back." She'd almost said stay, but she wouldn't stay without being married, and she wanted to be married in Texas, where all of her family was.

"I want you to come back," he said softly. "We're bound to have fights, but I think we've found an alternative for you to work here."

"Thank you for all the time and effort you put into making sure I would have an alternative here. What happens if I decide not to work?" She couldn't see it happening, but she had to ask.

"Then you don't work. I don't care either way. I just want you to be able to do what you've trained for, if you want to do it."

He picked up the key from the bar, and they walked toward the door together. "You know we're going to have to replace the bar with a barre, right?" she asked, wondering if he'd understand.

He nodded, his eyes full of humor. "That was one of the first things I thought of when I saw this building."

"I like your sense of humor, Michael Muir."

"I like everything about you, Heather McClain. Except maybe your temper. I'm not sure I like your temper."

She grinned. "Well, I need to be able to stand up for myself, right?"

"Yes, you do. Just not against me. I'm here for you . . . not against you."

After getting in the truck, she squeezed his hand. "I know. I really am sorry to be so moody. This is hard. I can leave everything I've ever known and everyone I've ever loved to marry a man who I believe I need to spend my life with . . . or I can stay home and let love pass me by." She wanted to kick herself for saying marriage, but he didn't seem to even react.

"I can see that it's a hard decision to make. I don't know that I could do it." He pulled out onto the street and drove toward the ranch.

"I wouldn't be able to walk to work here."

"That's true. But you would be dancing your heart out every day, and that would give you good exercise."

She was silent for a moment as she thought about it. "Are you excited to introduce me to the rest of your family tonight?"

"I am. I really do think you're going to love my sisters in particular. You'll have built-in friends if you move here. No pressure, but I guarantee they'll make you feel welcome and loved."

"Yeah, that makes everything so much easier." She made a face at him, and then regretted acting so childish. She was glad his eyes were on the road. "Is there enough snow for a snowman? I've never made one."

He pulled up in front of his mother's house and shut off the engine, staring at her in shock. "Never? How is that even possible?"

"I've lived in Texas my whole life. We get ice but not much snow. I've always wanted to build a snowman and maybe make a snow angel."

"Let's do it! Hang on, though. I need to tell Mom what we're doing, so she'll know her part in it all."

Heather frowned. "Why does your mother have a part?"

"You'll see." Michael ran to the door, yelled something to his mother, and then he walked back to Heather. "Let's find a good central spot. You start with a snowball . . ." He explained to her how snowmen were made, and they created their very own work of art right there in his mother's yard.

After eyeing their snowman for a moment, she took off her scarf to give it some color. "He's beautiful! The most beautiful snowman that has ever been!"

He grinned at her. She was so happy to be playing in the snow. "Now for snow angels."

Heather frowned. She'd been all for it before she lost her scarf. "What if snow goes down the back of my neck?"

"Then you'll get cold. It's snow. Come on." He found a patch of untouched snow and carefully got onto his back without messing it up. "You'll regret it if you don't do it!"

She knew he was right and carefully joined him. "All right. Now what?"

He didn't say anything about her not even knowing how to make a snow angel. "Move your arms and legs. Like this." He demonstrated, watching as she started doing the same. Then he showed her how to carefully get to her feet without messing up her creation. "There. Your first snow angel. It's magnificent!"

She tilted her head to one side, studying it. "I approve. I believe I like making snow angels."

Michael grinned and pulled her to him, kissing her softly.

Heather felt the snow falling onto her face, and her eyelashes felt wet against her cheeks. "I think I love snow."

"I hope you continue to love it. The first snow is always pretty and special. By April, we're all hating it." He took her hand and led her to the door. "Now it's time for Mom's part of playing in the snow."

He stomped and brushed the snow off him at the front door, and she followed suit. When they got inside the house, he led her to the kitchen, where his mother had fresh-baked chocolate chip cookies and hot chocolate topped with marshmallow cream.

Heather squealed and hugged Mrs. Muir. "Thank you! This is perfect for a snack after playing in the snow. I didn't even realize I was hungry until we stepped inside."

"Every first snowfall of the year, I would send the kids out to play, and I would make chocolate chip cookies and hot chocolate. It's a family tradition. And while this isn't our first snowfall of the year, it is yours, so I had to do it up right."

Heather sat at the table and pulled one of the mugs full of chocolate toward her, taking a sip. Michael laughed and reached over to rub the marshmallow off her top lip with his thumb. "There."

Her eyes locked on his, and she so badly wanted to kiss him, but she was fully aware of his mother sitting at the table with them, drinking her own hot chocolate. Instead, she turned her attention to Mrs. Muir. "Is there anything I can do to help with supper tonight?"

"Yup. Stay out of my way." The words were softened with a smile, but it was apparent that Mrs. Muir truly meant them. She had no desire to have anyone in her kitchen when she was preparing a feast for her family.

Heather nodded, a smile touching her lips. "So I either spend the rest of the day with Michael or I read some of those romance novels you mentioned."

Michael sighed. "I need to get back to work. Romance novels. Maybe you can go out and work with me tomorrow if you still want to. I think you should warm up after your fun in the snow before you plan to spend more time outside."

"You're going straight out."

He laughed. "Yes, but I'm an Idaho man. You're a Texas girl." Ignoring his mother, he dropped a kiss atop her head as he headed back outside. "I'll see you in a while."

Heather shrugged. "Where are those books?"

Chapter Ten

Heather had no trouble completely immersing herself in a novel by Jude Deveraux while she waited for supper. She sat in her room, in a big overstuffed chair in the corner, and she read and read. Finally, around five, there was a knock on her door. When she opened it, she saw Mrs. Muir.

"Enjoying your book?"

"I am. It's delightful!"

"Good. I thought I'd let you know that we'll be eating in about forty-five minutes. I assume you don't want your hair to be all flat from the snow."

Heather caught a glimpse of herself in the mirror over the dresser. She sighed. "Yeah, I think there are some things that need to be done about that."

"Come down when you're ready," Mrs. Muir told her.

Heather was a little nervous about meeting his sisters, because she knew just how snarky young women could be. She fixed her hair until it was as big as any self-respecting eighties woman would make her hair, and then she fixed her makeup. She wanted to look just perfect.

She changed into a pair of jeans and a nice pullover sweater, and then she was ready. Hurrying down the stairs, she went to the kitchen and found Mrs. Muir putting the finishing touches on supper. "Do you want to carry this into the dining room for me?" she asked, pointing to a big bowl of mashed potatoes.

For the next few minutes, Heather played kitchen lackey as she waited for the others to arrive.

The first to get there was Michael, accompanied by his brother Joshua. Joshua had a green aura around him that wasn't nearly as appealing as Michael's blue. "You must be Heather. I swear, you're all Michael has talked about since he got back from Texas."

"I hope he managed to say some good things," Heather said softly, a smile on her face.

"*Only* good things. It's good to meet such a perfect woman. I hear you have sisters!"

Heather laughed. "I have six sisters. Do you want to go all the way to Texas to meet them?"

"Not particularly!"

She grinned at him. "Well, that's where my sisters are."

Michael walked closer to her and wrapped his arm around her shoulders. "We looked at the old saloon in town today, and she agrees it would be good for a dance studio."

"Wonderful. Just know we're all willing to do the work if you decide you want to renovate," Joshua said.

"Thank you!" Heather was already liking this family, and Joshua looked a lot like Michael except for the strange hue to his skin.

The door opened then, and in rushed another man who looked like the others. She realized then she didn't know his name, so she waited for someone to introduce them.

Michael looked at his brother. "Amos, this is Heather. Heather, this is Amos."

"Nice to meet you, Amos." Heather was very aware of Michael's arm locked around her shoulders. It was obvious he was keeping her from his brothers. She wanted to laugh, because neither of his brothers was right for her. Amos had a yellow hue to his skin.

"You too. With as high on a pedestal as Michael has you, I hope it didn't hurt when you fell off."

"My angel wings saved me," she quipped, winking at Amos, who laughed.

"Keep her!" Amos told his brother. "She's what you need."

"I agree."

When the door opened again, it was a woman with a man and two children in tow. "Karen, this is Heather. Heather, this is my sister Karen. Her two little ones are Katie and Kurt. Her husband is Ken."

"It's nice to meet you, Karen."

"You too! I'm so excited you're finally here. When we first heard that Michael was staying in Texas because of some girl he'd met, I wanted to fly down there immediately to meet you, but that wouldn't have been smart. I would have had to find a sitter . . ."

Heather grinned. "I would have felt like a zoo specimen. I'm glad you waited."

"So . . . if you open that dance studio . . . what are the ages you'll take?"

"I do two and up at my studio at home. Are you wanting to put them both in dance?"

"I was thinking I would. It wouldn't be a bad thing for Kurt to learn to be graceful."

"Do you live in town?" Heather asked, already liking this sister and wanting to get to know her better.

"I do. Ken is the high school football coach. We sure need a cheerleading coach . . ."

"Well, we'll see if I end up coming here. If I do, we can discuss it."

Karen glanced over her shoulder at Ken. "That's a yes!"

The door opened, which thrilled Heather, because she had no idea how to respond. In came a petite brunette with a huge blond man. "Everyone, this is Scott. Scott, this is my sister, Karen, my brothers Michael, Amos, and Joshua, and my mother, Berniece. Oh, and this is Karen's husband, Ken, and her two, Katie and Kurt. And you must be Heather!"

Heather smiled at the newcomer. "It's nice to meet you, Isabelle." She felt Michael's gaze on her, and she gave a slight shake of her head. She hoped that he would know that meant Isabelle didn't belong with Scott.

"It's time to eat!" Mrs. Muir announced. "Let's all head into the dining room, and we'll play Trivial Pursuit after."

During dinner, there was a lot of joking and teasing. It reminded Heather of a family meal with her own family, and that was good. She felt right at home.

Heather hadn't been in this room yet, and over the table was a picture of the family all together. Michael couldn't have been more than sixteen. Mr. and Mrs. Muir were in the center in the back, and their hues blended perfectly. She truly had the man of her dreams, and she'd given up years of their lives together. It made her realize she didn't want that with Michael. When he asked her to marry him, her answer would definitely be yes.

As soon as the meal was over, Heather stood up to help clear the table. Despite the objections of the other women there, she helped, and when the table was cleaned off and all of the food put away, they all sat down to play Trivial Pursuit.

Michael stood up. "Picking teams. I'm a captain. Amos and Josh are captains. And Kurt, you be a captain. I'm picking first, because I'm the bossiest, and I pick Heather."

"That's a surprise," Isabelle said, rolling her eyes. "Who didn't see that coming?"

Everyone ignored Isabelle, and it was obvious that she was usually ignored, because she had no trouble with it. Once the teams were divvied up, they rolled the dice to see who would go first. Berniece decided to be the referee instead of playing because the teams would be uneven, and she knew her children *needed* a referee.

For Michael and Heather's first question, they were asked who composed the ballet *Swan Lake*. Michael immediately looked stumped, but Heather calmly answered Tchaikovsky. When Isabelle, who had read the card, told them they were right, Michael calmly looked at Heather. "Would you marry me?"

Heather swallowed hard, before nodding. "You know what? I think I will."

Michael pulled out the ring he'd had in his pocket all day and held it out to her, and she gave him her hand, so he could slip it on her finger. Then he gathered her to him and kissed her in front of everyone.

"Romantic proposal," Isabelle said with a groan.

Heather grinned. "It was perfect for me. Surrounded by family. What more could I ask for?"

"You should make him get down on one knee!" Karen said. "I'd love to see that!"

"I don't think that's necessary," Heather said softly. She rested her head on Michael's shoulder, thrilled.

"When?" Michael asked.

"Christmas. It's always been my favorite holiday. Let's have a Christmas wedding."

"In Texas?" he asked, knowing that would be her preference.

She nodded. "I want all of my sisters there. And your family, too!"

Karen looked at Ken. "I have a feeling we're going to Texas for Christmas."

"I guess we are," Ken responded.

The game was completely derailed as they all started talking about wedding plans. Mrs. Muir was excited to be part of it, and she insisted that she go to Texas a week before the wedding to help put finishing touches on everything.

As everyone else talked, Heather and Michael drifted into the living room and sat together on the couch, snuggled close. "Are you sure you'll be ready to marry that quickly?" he asked. "I'm not complaining, because I want you here forever starting right this second, but I don't want to do all the work to get ready and then have you realized you're not prepared."

"Don't worry about me. You just get my studio ready and plan to be in Texas for Christmas. I'll take care of the rest."

"Can my mom stay with you? She's not kidding about going a week early."

"Oh, don't worry about that. She can stay with my mom, and I have a feeling they're going to be best friends really fast."

"That works." He pressed a kiss to her forehead. "I can't believe we're really getting married."

"I can. I knew you were my destiny from the moment I set eyes on you."

"You and me both. I love you, Heather. I plan to make you the happiest woman alive."

"And I love you. I plan to make you the most tormented man alive."

He laughed at that. "I'm already there."

Epilogue

Heather stood in the center of a circle comprised entirely of her sisters. It was the night before her wedding, and she was supposed to be having a bachelorette party, but they'd voted instead to watch movies and talk. So far, no movies had been put into the VCR.

Heather finally decided to broach the subject that had been bothering her for months. "Do you guys remember when Dad called us all over to the house to look at his new cell phone? And when the power went out? Did anyone else feel . . . well . . . changed after that outage?"

"I did!" Jessica said. "Weird stuff has been happening to me ever since. I keep having dreams that stuff is happening, and then I find out it happened at the exact moment I dreamed it!"

Heather grinned. "I can look at two people and tell if they're meant to be together or if they should leave each other alone."

"That's so cool!" Gaylynn said. "I've gotten to the point that when people tell me stories in counseling sessions—or any other time for that matter—I can picture what they're saying . . . like, I see a playback of whatever they're talking about. And if they're lying, I see what's really happening!"

"Oh, that's neat!" Heather said.

"I can touch someone and know exactly what's wrong with them," Rebekah said. "It's so weird!"

"I can touch *things* and know what's wrong with them!" Tracy said. "If someone brings the dealership a used car, I can touch it and know how much the repair costs are going to be. It's coming in really handy!"

"That would be great for your job!" Heather shook her head. "We all changed, didn't we?"

Candice bit her lip. "I can sense the weather. Like, I can tell you exactly what weather is going to happen for the next week." She grinned at Heather. "Don't worry, it's not going to rain on your wedding day."

"That's not what the weatherman said!" Heather frowned. "Are you sure?"

"I'm so much better than a weatherman. I'm always right!"

All of the sisters turned their attentions to Marti then. The baby of the family, who had always been coddled. What was her power?

"I know when things will happen. I've looked it up, and they call me a precognitive. It's crazy, but I know so many different things. I mean, I'm not shown everything, but I'm shown enough that I feel safe to say I'm a precog."

Heather shook her head. "Has anyone told Mom and Dad?"

There was a chorus of nos. "Do you think we should?" Heather asked. "I mean, those things happen in our family. No one would be terribly surprised, especially since there are seven of us."

Marti frowned. "I like having it just our secret, you know? It feels good that we have this special thing bonding all of us together as sisters."

Jessica nodded. "I agree. I think it should just be us knowing . . . at least for now. If we need to tell the parents and the rest of the family at some point, we will, but for now . . . I feel good knowing that it's just us."

Heather looked around, seeing that all of her sisters were nodding. "Well, I did tell Michael, just so you all know. I knew we were meant to be together from the moment I set eyes on him."

"As long as the rest of us can borrow that power from you when we need it, I think that's perfectly fine," Gaylynn said with a wink.

They all laughed. When they'd quieted down, Heather said, "I want you to know how much it means to me that all of you are here for my wedding. That you're all standing up with me. I know it's going to be the biggest wedding party in the history of wedding parties, but I don't care, because my sisters will be there with me."

Marti yelled, "Group hug!" and they all swarmed around Heather, hugging her at the center of their enormous hug.

"I feel squished!" Heather finally complained.

"Such a tender moment, and she ruins it," Jessica said, shaking her head.

"Well, would you want to be squished?" Tracy asked.

"I wouldn't," Candice said.

"Me neither!" Rebekah agreed. "I think we all need to not squish our sister before her wedding day."

"Are you nervous?" Marti asked softly.

Heather shook her head. "I know he's the right man for me. I know I belong with him, and his family is amazing. I mean, I hate to leave Texas, because I have always been here with the people I love, but now there are new people I love." She took a deep breath. "What I'm trying to say is I'm going to miss you all terribly, but I'll still visit and y'all can visit." She brushed away a tear. "I love you guys."

This time Marti didn't have to call for the group hug. It was spontaneous.

INTERESTED IN READING more by Kirsten Osbourne? Subscribe to her newsletter for updates on new books! Text "Bob" to 42828.

With more than 200 books out, Kirsten loves to write down stories about people she makes up in her head. Would you like to give feedback? kirstenosbourne@gmail.com or for a complete list of books go to kirstenandmorganna.com.

Don't miss out!

Visit the website below and you can sign up to receive emails whenever Kirsten Osbourne publishes a new book. There's no charge and no obligation.

https://books2read.com/r/B-A-VSFD-WWYTB

BOOKS 2 READ

Connecting independent readers to independent writers.